W9-BPK-325

At Issue

| Fast Food

Other Books in the At Issue Series:

At Issue

Fast Food

Roman Espejo, Book Editor

GREENHAVEN PRESS
A part of Gale, Cengage Learning

GALE
CENGAGE Learning™

Detroit • New York • San Francisco • New Haven, Conn • Waterville, Maine • London

Christine Nasso, *Publisher*
Elizabeth Des Chenes, *Managing Editor*

© 2009 Greenhaven Press, a part of Gale, Cengage Learning.

Gale and Greenhaven Press are registered trademarks used herein under license.

For more information, contact:
Greenhaven Press
27500 Drake Rd.
Farmington Hills, MI 48331-3535
Or you can visit our Internet site at gale.cengage.com

For product information and technology assistance, contact us at

Gale Customer Support, 1-800-877-4253
For permission to use material from this text or product, submit all requests online at www.cengage.com/permissions

Further permissions questions can be emailed to permissionrequest@cengage.com

Articles in Greenhaven Press anthologies are often edited for length to meet page requirements. In addition, original titles of these works are changed to clearly present the main thesis and to explicitly indicate the author's opinion. Every effort is made to ensure that Greenhaven Press accurately reflects the original intent of the authors. Every effort has been made to trace the owners of copyrighted material.

Cover photograph © Images.com/Corbis.

LIBRARY OF CONGRESS CATALOGING-IN-PUBLICATION DATA

Fast food / Roman Espejo, book editor.
 p. cm. -- (At issue)
 Includes bibliographical references and index.
 ISBN-13: 978-0-7377-4300-5 (hardcover)
 ISBN-13: 978-0-7377-4299-2 (pbk.)
 1. Convenience foods. I. Espejo, Roman, 1977-
 TX370.F37 2009
 642'.1--dc22

                                                    2008052832

Printed in the United States of America
1 2 3 4 5 6 7 13 12 11 10 09

Contents

Introduction

In 2004's shocking documentary *Super Size Me*, writer and director Morgan Spurlock ate food purchased only at McDonald's three times a day for thirty days. He tried everything on the menu at least once and "supersized" his meals each time it was offered. By the end of the experiment, Spurlock reportedly ate the amount of McDonald's a typical American should eat in eight years. Consequently, to various doctors' dismay, the certifiably healthy thirty-two-year-old gained almost twenty-five pounds, experienced depression and other mood changes, had heart palpitations, and even sustained liver damage.

Super Size Me inflamed the roiling debate surrounding fast food's alleged link to rising rates of obesity, heart disease, and diabetes as well as heightened cholesterol levels in Americans, and it even earned an Academy Award nomination. Furthermore, after the documentary's release, McDonald's ceased supersizing its meals and added salad and fruit options to its menu, but denied that *Super Size Me* had any impact on these changes. Other restaurant franchises, such Wendy's, Burger King, and Chick-fil-A, followed suit, and similar so-called health-conscious items have become mainstays at their outlets.

In June 2008, another man who ate mostly at McDonald's also made headlines—but for becoming *slimmer*. In six months, Chris Coleson of Virginia downsized his five-foot, eight-inch frame from 276 to 199 pounds—shrinking his waist from fifty to thirty-six inches—by eating McDonald's salads, wraps, chicken sandwiches, and apple dippers (without the caramel sauce on the side). Sometimes, the then forty-two-year-old crumbled a hamburger patty into a salad from the menu. His wife, Patricia Sumner, was skeptical of his Golden Arches diet; he chose the burger franchise out of convenience.

But as her husband began to lose weight, Sumner joined him on his "McFit" diet and shed thirty pounds herself.

McDonald's headquarters did not officially comment on Coleson's weight loss but told ABC News that they "applaud his efforts and his results." Nonetheless, the McFit weight-loss plan may not receive Jenny Craig's or Weight Watcher's stamp of approval. Coleson skipped breakfast and ate only twice a day at McDonald's, dramatically reducing his daily caloric intake from an excessive five thousand calories to fourteen hundred calories, which many dieticians would deem unhealthy for a man of his stature. In fact, Christine Gerbstadt, spokesperson for the American Dietetic Association, insists that he was on a "starvation diet."

Both Spurlock and Coleson took fast-food consumption to the extreme, and their temporary all-McDonald's diets do not resemble average eating habits. But their experiments underline the following question: How accountable are fast-food restaurants for their customers' health? Spurlock was impelled to examine this in *Super Size Me* partly because of a dismissed 2003 lawsuit in which two New York girls claimed that they had become addicted to McDonald's Chicken McNuggets, fries, and other menu items without being warned of the food's harmful effects, including their own obesity and diabetes. In fact, some studies suggest that consuming foods high in fat and sugar trigger natural opioids in the brain, simulating highs and withdrawals that are chemically similar to that created by heroin and cocaine. Yet others, like former *Addiction* editor James Griffith Edwards, are cynical of such addiction comparisons: "Whether a burger habit can be regarded as an addiction depends on how you define 'addiction.' The difference is not a qualitative one but a quantitative one. I am quite fond of dark chocolate, but it is not going to destroy my life like a heroin addiction."

As for Coleson's McFit diet, some experts support any efforts by fast-food franchises to take some responsibility for the health of customers like him—customers who may eat at restaurants like McDonald's because of their convenience or low prices—by providing leafier and leaner alternatives to burgers, fries, and other fast-food staples. Kevin Huggins, assistant nutrition and food science professor at Alabama's Auburn University, observes, "It used to be just a burger, fries, and a drink. Now you can get fruit and salads, and portion size has gotten a lot better." With young people's diets in mind, which are often lacking in fresh fruits and vegetables, Huggins states that "we tell students . . . to choose the colors. The more colors, the more vitamins, minerals, and antioxidants." Some critics, however, buck the notion that McDonald's and KFC could ever be places for teaching healthful eating habits and assert that fast-food companies should not stray from their path to success. For instance, *Brand Strategy* editor Ruth Mortimer claims, "In a time of global obesity concerns, it makes sense for a fast-food chain to start serving something less calorie loaded. That's certainly true, but when does 'responding to consumer needs' become 'undermining your core brand ethos and offering?'"

McDonald's may have stopped clocking the billions of burgers they serve every year, and the brand is becoming synonymous with its sundry salads and wraps. Still, with worldwide obesity on the rise, fast-food franchises will continue to dish out controversy. In *At Issue: Fast Food*, nutritionists, gourmets, and activists alike bring their views of the "all-American meal" to the plate.

1

Fast Food Is Linked to Obesity and Other Serious Health Problems

Seth Stern

Seth Stern is a staff writer at The Christian Science Monitor.

Despite the fact that nutritional information about fast food is readily available, many fast food chains are taking the blame for the rise in obesity and other health problems across the nation. Some lawyers are considering the possibility that fast food chains could be held accountable for the health consequences of eating their food. The chains could also be responsible for the effects of their potentially misleading advertising, especially to children. These advertising messages can lead people to overeat, which is one of the reasons behind the obesity problem.

For decades, Caesar Barber ate hamburgers four or five times a week at his favorite fast-food restaurants, visits that didn't end even after his first heart attack.

But his appetite for fast food didn't stop Mr. Barber, who is 5 foot 10 and weighs 272 pounds, from suing four chains last month, claiming they contributed to his health problems by serving fatty foods.

Legal Matters

Even the most charitable legal experts give Barber little chance of succeeding. But his suit is just the latest sign that the Big Mac may eventually rival Big Tobacco as public health enemy No. 1 in the nation's courts.

Seth Stern, "Fast-Food Restaurants Face Legal Grilling," *The Christian Science Monitor*, August 8, 2002. Reproduced by permission from *Christian Science Monitor* (www.csmonitor.com).

Lawyers who successfully challenged cigarette manufacturers have joined with nutritionists to explore whether the producers of all those supersize fries and triple cheeseburgers can be held liable for America's bulging waistlines.

Prompted by reports that the nation's obesity is getting worse, lawyers as well as nutrition, marketing, and industry economics experts will come together at a conference at Northeastern University in Boston to discuss possible legal strategies.

Obesity can be linked to some 300,000 deaths and $117 billion in health care costs a year.

They're looking at whether food industry marketing—particularly messages aimed at kids—may be misleading or downright deceptive under consumer protection laws, says Richard Daynard, a Northeastern law professor and chair of its Tobacco Products Liability Project. They'll also consider the more complex question of whether the producers of fatty foods—and even the public schools that sell them—should be held responsible for the health consequences of eating them.

A Toxic Food Environment

Medical professionals argue that too much unhealthy food is sold by using tempting messages that encourage overeating. "People are exposed to a toxic food environment," says Kelly Brownell of Yale's Center for Eating and Weight Disorders. "It really is an emergency."

The figures are certainly startling. Obesity can be linked to some 300,000 deaths and $117 billion in health care costs a year, a report by the Surgeon General found [in 2001].

Such numbers prompted President [George W.] Bush to launch his own war on fat this summer [in 2002], calling on all Americans to get 30 minutes of physical activity each day.

But fast-food industry representatives are quick to say, "Don't just blame us." Steven Anderson, president of the National Restaurant Association, a trade group, says attorneys who attempt to compare the health risk of tobacco with those of fast food are following a "tortuous and twisted" logic.

"All of these foods will fit into [the] diet of most Americans with proper moderation and balance," he says.

To be sure, there are big differences between tackling food and tobacco. Any amount of tobacco consumption is dangerous but everyone has to eat, Mr. Daynard says. And few if any foods are inherently toxic.

What's more, while there were only four or five tobacco manufacturers, there are thousands of food manufacturers and restaurants serving some 320,000 different products, says Marion Nestle, a professor of nutrition and food studies at New York University.

People usually smoke one brand of cigarette. They eat in many restaurants and eat the same foods at home. That makes it almost impossible to prove that a person's obesity or health problems are caused by a particular food or restaurant.

As a result, suits such as Barber's that attempt to pin the blame for weight-related problems on specific plaintiffs will run into difficulty in court, says Steven Sugarman, a law professor at the University of California, Berkeley. Suits by state attorneys general to try to recover the cost of treating obese patients, a tactic that's worked with tobacco, also could prove tough.

Deceptive Advertising

That's why lawyers are focusing on more modest suits aimed at advertising and marketing techniques, says John Banzhaf III, a George Washington University law professor who helped initiate the tobacco litigation three decades ago.

For example, students in one of Professor Banzhaf's courses helped sue McDonald's [in 2000] for advertising its french fries as vegetarian even though the company continued to use beef fat in their preparation. The company agreed to donate $10 million to Hindu and vegetarian groups as part of a settlement.

But only in the past few months has Banzhaf considered similar suits as part of a concerted strategy to sue the food industry for false or deceptive advertising as a way of fighting Americans' obesity.

State consumer-protection laws require sellers to disclose clearly all important facts about their products. Just as a sweater manufacturer should disclose that it may shrink in the wash, Banzhaf says fast-food companies might have an obligation to disclose that a meal has more fat than the recommended daily allowance.

Such class-action suits on behalf of people deceived by advertisements could recover the amounts customers spent on the food items but not money spent on related health costs.

As with tobacco, marketing aimed at kids will be a particular focus of Banzhaf and his coalition of lawyers and nutritionists.

"Everybody is looking at children as the vulnerable point in this," says Dr. Nestle. She says she's received "loads" of e-mails and calls from plaintiff lawyers interested in advice since publishing "Food Politics," a book critical of the food industry's marketing and its dominant role in shaping nutritional guidelines.

"While they know a quarter pounder is not a health food, a lot of people would be surprised to learn it uses up a whole day of calories for women."

At a meeting in Boston [August 2002], Banzhaf said attorneys talked about suing Massachusetts school districts that sell fast food in their cafeterias or stock soda in their vending machines. These suits would be based on the legal notion that schools have a higher "duty of care" than restaurants.

Fast-food restaurant chains, for their part, say they're not hiding what's in their food. At Burger King, for example, nutritional information is supposed to be posted in every dining room. And on its website, Wendy's lists 15 categories of information about its products, including total fat and calories for everything from the whole sandwich down to the pickles.

Nutritionists say that the information doesn't put the calories in a context people can understand.

"While they know a quarter pounder is not a health food, a lot of people would be surprised to learn it uses up a whole day of calories for women," says Margo Wootan of the Center for Science in the Public Interest in Washington.

Banzhaf acknowledges that litigation alone won't get Americans in better shape. He'd like nutritional information on the fast-food menu boards and wrappers or even health warnings similar to the ones now required on cigarettes.

Still, Banzhaf says litigation will put producers of fatty foods on notice. "When we first proposed smoker suits, people laughed too."

2

The Link Between Fast Food and Obesity Is Distorted

J. Eric Oliver

J. Eric Oliver is a political science professor at the University of Chicago and author of Fat Politics: The Real Story Behind America's Obesity Epidemic.

The 2004 documentary Super Size Me, *in which director Morgan Spurlock ate McDonald's fast food exclusively for a month—gaining twenty-six pounds and risking liver damage—placed chain restaurants and food manufacturers under fire. The link seems obvious, but a closer look reveals that super-sized meals are not the culprit of America's growing obesity dilemma. On the contrary, American cuisine has always had traditionally large portions; in fact, Americans are dining out more than ever, but they are not consuming bigger meals. What has dramatically changed in the American diet is the consumption of snacks and sodas. In the United States, calories from snacking have jumped from 13 to 25 percent since the 1970s, while soda-drinking has jumped 130 percent, making it a dietary staple despite its empty calories and lack of nutritional value.*

One of the surprise movie hits of 2004 was a low-budget documentary, *Super Size Me*, in which the director, Morgan Spurlock, recorded what happened when he ate nothing but McDonald's fast-food, three times a day, for a month.

J. Eric Oliver, "Food and Weight Gain: Super Sized Misconceptions," in *Fat Politics: The Real Story Behind America's Obesity Epidemic.* New York: Oxford University Press, 2006, pp. 122–24, 131–134. Copyright © 2006 by J. Eric Oliver. All rights reserved. Reproduced by permission of Oxford University Press, Inc.

Within two weeks of starting his McDonald's diet, Spurlock's health started to decline—his cholesterol and blood pressure shot up and his doctor started to worry if he was doing long-term damage to his liver. In addition, Spurlock seemed to have a negative psychological reaction to his new diet—he became moody, depressed, and agitated. Like any addict, Spurlock's moods elevated and crashed between each McDonald's "fix." And, most important from the film's perspective, he gained twenty-six pounds. The film offers Spurlock's own personal degeneration as a metaphor for America's obesity epidemic—Spurlock went from a model of health and fitness to an overweight lout, due in large part to the nefarious efforts of McDonald's to super size his value meals.

Americans Are Suspicious

Audiences ate it up. The film, which went on to become one of the highest grossing documentaries of all time, seemed to strike a nerve in the popular consciousness. Many Americans are growing increasingly suspicious that the foods we are eating are making us fat. Many, including Spurlock, lay the blame squarely on the shoulders of America's major food and restaurant companies. From obesity experts such as Kelly Brownell and Marion Nestle to best-selling writers such as Eric Schlosser (author of *Fast Food Nation*), numerous critics are accusing the major food manufacturers and restaurants for plying an unsuspecting public with too much fattening fare. Others, including writers Greg Critser and Michael Pollan, take a broader perspective and see McDonald's merely as a middleman. They blame the U.S. government for subsidizing corn, which, in turn, allows food makers to flood the market with inexpensive sweeteners and food additives. In their view, the only reason that McDonald's is able to super size your meal is because the government makes it so cheap for them to do so. Then there are those who blame obesity on the government's nutritional recommendations. According to this theory, Americans started to gain weight in the late 1970s because they were following the government's advice to substitute dietary fat with carbohydrates. Ironically, it was the very effort to eat better that has contributed to our growing weight.

Food is no longer about sustenance or even sociability; it is about amusement and self-medication.

At first glance, these charges seem to encapsulate the real political story of obesity in America. Much like the allegations leveled against Big Tobacco a decade ago [in the mid 1990s], the indictment of Big Food suggests that corporate interests, political lobbying, and bureaucratic ineptitude have taken precedence over America's health. Americans are getting fat because a handful of major food companies is shaping government policy and bending consumer preference so that we eat more. Given the billions of dollars that McDonald's and other food companies spend on advertising each year and the political influence of the food lobby, these accusations are quite understandable. But while these charges have some elements of fact, they are much like the proverbial blind men trying to describe an elephant; each depicts an aspect of the problem, but misses the much larger picture regarding our diet, weight, and health.

Our Drug of Choice

In fact, Americans are not consuming more carbohydrates and trans fats because McDonald's is super sizing our dinners. Nor is our diet changing because Uncle Sam is subsidizing corn. Rather, Americans are eating poorly because of a much more fundamental change in *how* we eat, specifically, the rise of snacking. In fact, the amount we eat and drink between meals accounts for nearly all the growth in our consumption of carbohydrates and fats over the past thirty years. Perhaps the biggest source of America's recent weight gain and sugary diet is not so much the value "meal" but the simple snack.

The reason that Americans snack so much is because the free market has finally caught up with American food culture. As America's agricultural sector industrialized and consolidated, it began creating products that both eliminate the need for cooking and promote individualized eating. This, in turn, has redefined the American meal, both freeing us to eat when and where we want, but also giving food new purposes. With snacking, food is no longer about sustenance or even sociability; it is about amusement and self-medication. We now eat to relieve our stress, to alleviate our boredom, or to simply make ourselves feel better. Food, in short, has become our drug of choice. And the types of foods that are best suited for these psychological tasks are the very ones that cause us so many health problems, that is, sweets, fats, and refined carbohydrates. In other words, the ultimate source of the changing American diet goes beyond McDonald's, corn syrup, or the food pyramid; the ultimate source is the American way of life. . . .

Increased Portion Sizes

Although America's food industry may not suffer from a lack of critics, few have been more forceful, persistent, or notable than Kelly Brownell, a psychologist and director of the Yale Center for Eating and Weight Disorders, and Marion Nestle, a professor of nutrition at New York University. Brownell and Nestle have written books, made headlines, and been lauded by *Time* magazine as America's "obesity warriors" for their efforts to tie Americans' growing weights to the way a handful of large food companies market and sell their products. If America's obesity epidemic has a single cause, it is, in their eyes, from the corporate malfeasance of its food makers.

According to Brownell and Nestle, Big Food (meaning the major food companies including Kraft, General Mills, PepsiCo, Coca-Cola, ConAgra, Tyson Food, Mars, Sara Lee, Heinz, and IBP) has created a "toxic environment" that is causing Americans to get fat. These companies disguise or label food as "healthy" that is really filled with sugars, fats, and little nutritional value. They have targeted children with thousands of commercials featuring cartoon characters and celebrities encouraging them to eat unhealthy foods. And, most important, they have packaged foods in larger sizes, which, in the name of value, encourages Americans to eat more than they otherwise would. Brownell writes, "Portion size increases conspire to drive up food intake and appear to contribute to increasing obesity. Food companies claim to 'provide people what they want' and take no responsibility for manipulating portion sizes in ways that increase overall eating."

Americans are consuming more calories, but it does not seem to come from super sizing their meals.

From Nestle's perspective, the biggest problem with these super size portions is that most of us are poor estimators of how much we need to eat. In fact, she claims the food industry has completely warped what Americans now see as a recommended serving size. Most Americans think a serving size is between two and three times larger than the official USDA [United States Department of Agriculture] designations. Super sized portions also encourage us to eat more by influencing our levels of hunger and satiation. For example, nutrition researchers have demonstrated that when people are given larger portions of food, they will eat more before they feel satisfied. Partly this is because we get pleasure from food—the satisfaction of eating, particularly foods high in sugars and fats, resonates in our brains—and partly this is because we often feel compelled to "clean our plates" in order not to be wasteful. Considering the millions of value meals served at fast-food restaurants every day, Americans allegedly are being lured into consuming more calories than they might otherwise do. Nestle concludes, "Taken together, advertising, convenience, larger portions, and the added nutrients in food otherwise high in fat, sugar, and salt all contribute to an environment that promotes 'eat more.'"

A Way of Life

Once again, at first glance, Brownell's and Nestle's charges seem to have a lot of merit. Over the past forty years, America has transformed from a society where most people prepared their own meals from scratch to one where most meals are either prepackaged or eaten outside of the home. One need only look at the growing number of fast-food restaurants, the ever increasing portion sizes in those restaurants, or the size and type of foods available in supermarkets to believe that food companies are responsible for America's weight gain. Today, Americans spend about half their food dollars at restaurants or on take-out meals, a rate double that of a generation ago and on any given day, half of all Americans will get at least one meal from a restaurant. The result, according to the Brownell and Nestle, is that America is growing obese.

Yet, once again, these charges miss the larger picture. To begin with, there is little indication that America's mealtime behaviors are being manipulated by the nefarious machinations of a few profit-hungry food conglomerates cajoling them into eating larger portions. Yes, Americans are consuming more calories, but it does not seem to come from super sizing their meals. In fact, larger portion sizes at meals seem to have very little to do with the increase in calorie consumption within the United States. For example, Nestle's argument on portion size contributing to obesity rests almost entirely on data about the manufacture of foods, she has no data on whether people are actually consuming larger portions during meals. If you look at the real data on how Americans eat, you'll see that the preoccupation with portion sizes misses the real culprit behind America's weight gain—snacking.

Snacking and Drinking

A generation ago, most Americans limited their daily food consumption to three meals and if they did eat between meals it was likely to be a piece of fruit or something easily consumed. Today, the average adult eats the equivalent of four meals a day and children eat close to five, much more than in 1970. According to the calculations of Harvard economist David Cutler and his colleagues, in the mid-1970s, men consumed about 2,080 calories per day and women consumed roughly 1,515 calories per day. The biggest meal for both sexes was dinner, followed by lunch and then breakfast. Americans only got about 13 percent of their calories from snacking, a relatively small percentage. Today, men and women are getting almost 25 percent of their daily calories from snacking, the caloric equivalent of a full meal a generation ago. The average American male consumes more than 500 calories a day from snacks, the average female more than 346 calories a day. Even more interesting is that the calories from dinner have actually declined over the past several decades. Men and women are actually eating smaller dinners on average than they did thirty years ago. Although Americans may be eating out more and restaurants may be serving larger portions, Americans are not eating larger meals.

To suddenly blame the food industry for serving larger portion sizes is to ignore the fact that many Americans have been eating large meals for centuries.

What Americans are doing more of is snacking and drinking high-calorie beverages. Americans spend more than 38 billion dollars a year on snack foods, more than what they spend on higher education. Of course snacking itself does not necessarily lead to weight gain or health problems, depending on what is eaten. But Americans are snacking more on foods that are high in calories and low in nutritional value, such as cookies, chips, and candies. Over the past twenty years, sales of high-salt, high-calorie snack foods have skyrocketed, while that of fruits and vegetables (excluding potatoes) has only increased marginally.

Nowhere is the prevalence of high-calorie snack food more evident than in the accelerating growth of soft drink consumption, particularly by children. Since the late 1970s, Americans' soft drink consumption has increased by more than 130 percent. The average American drinks more than forty-four gallons of soft drinks a year and soft drinks comprise about one-fifth of their dietary sugar. This increase is particularly sharp among children. Soft drinks have now replaced milk for most children as a dietary staple and are the third most common *breakfast* food. The typical American teenage boy has at least three soft drink servings in a day—the equivalent of twenty teaspoons of sugar.

Americans Are Big Eaters

It is drinking and snacking, more than anything else, that have been responsible for changing the way we eat. And upon reflection, this makes sense. In the hoopla over obesity and the large value meals served in restaurants, most critics seem to forget that American culinary culture has always been distinguished by large portion sizes. As food historian Harvey Levenstein notes, "To nineteenth-century observers, the major differences between the American and British diets could usually be summed up in one word: abundance. Virtually every foreign visitor who wrote about American eating habits expressed amazement, shock, and even disgust at the quantity of food consumed." What was not consumed was generally saved. Products including Tupperware and plastic wrap were developed precisely in response to the bounty of leftovers that were coming from the large American dinners. To suddenly blame the food industry for serving larger portion sizes is to ignore the fact that many Americans have been eating large meals for centuries.

Thus, while the super size portions in American restaurants may seem like a convenient target, they do not explain why Americans are eating more. If we want to understand why Americans are eating so much between meals, and why, in particular, we are snacking on so many fatty and sugary foods, we need to look at the more fundamental processes that are shaping how we eat. In short, we need to understand the logic of food production in the United States.

3

The Fast-Food Industry Intentionally Markets Unhealthy Food to Children

Janice Shaw Crouse

Janice Shaw Crouse is the Senior Fellow at the Beverly LaHaye Institute, which is the think tank for Concerned Women for America. The Beverly LaHaye Institute is a conservative organization that conducts research on contemporary issues in order to create and confirm policy positions.

One of the driving forces behind the large increase in childhood obesity over the past three decades is advertising. Fast food chains spend more than $3 million a year on television advertising that targets children. These advertisements sometimes include cartoon characters that are particularly of interest to children. Many of these companies also have interactive Web sites that children can visit. These sites not only promote the companies' products, but they are also unregulated, unlike television advertising.

Lately, there has been a lot of talk about childhood obesity. As facts are accumulating, concern is mounting. The tipping point came with the realization that in the past three decades the rate of American children who are either overweight or obese increased by 300 percent—the obesity rate for preschoolers and teens tripled and, for elementary school kids, the obesity rate quadrupled.

No wonder. While children are consuming more "empty" calories, they are getting less exercise. In many communities,

Janice Shaw Crouse, "Children Are Eating the Fat of Our Land," Concerned Women for America, February 19, 2008. Reproduced by permission.

children cannot walk or ride bicycles to schools. M
have eliminated recess and physical education from
day. At home, the children are watching more tel
playing video games for longer and longer times during the
day. Twenty-six percent of American youth watch four or
more hours of television a day.

Television Advertising

Numerous experts in the fields of pediatrics and public health
have identified advertising, especially television advertising, as
one of the "most pernicious" factors driving the alarming increases in childhood obesity. Sadly, half of all advertising time
on children's shows is food advertising. The Advertising Coalition reports that $10 billion to $15 billion is spent annually
on food advertising targeting children—over $3 billion a year
on fast food advertising alone.

*In a three-month monitoring project, over 12 million
children visited websites promoting food and beverage
products.*

There is no question that the nation's children are pro-
foundly influenced by the extent and type of this advertising
and that it represents a significant public health threat to children. Some advertisers are taking steps to counter the ava-
lanche of television advertising for unhealthy foods. While
these actions are laudable, they are not entirely voluntary;
some lawsuits are threatened by advocacy groups, and pressure is mounting from the FCC [Federal Communications
Commission], Congress and the public.

Recently, ten of the largest food and beverage companies,
including McDonald's, General Mills and Kellogg's, promised
that half of their advertising directed to children would promote healthier food and encourage more active lifestyles.
Kraft foods promised to conform their advertising to good

nutritional standards. The Kellogg Company announced that it would phase out advertising its products to children under 12 unless the foods meet specific nutrition guidelines for calories, sugar, fat and sodium.

One of the sticking points of advertising in children's programming is having program characters and hosts featured in commercials that run during the program in which they appear. Another is the practice of having cartoon characters featured in commercials during a children's program. Kellogg promised to stop using licensed characters and branded toys to promote its foods unless they meet the nutritional guidelines.

Healthier Messages Fall Short

Some broadcasters (Disney, for example) are incorporating healthier messages into their children's programming. Such actions are necessary to turn around the onslaught of advertising of products that provide poor nutrition to children. To date, however, these efforts are falling short of what is needed to have enough educational and informational broadcasting to help children. Nor are those efforts enough to limit the overwhelming amount of advertising that potentially harms children.

In another symbolic action, Nickelodeon has joined with the Boys and Girls Clubs of America and the Alliance for a Healthier Generation over the past four years to sponsor a "Let's Just Play" campaign. In addition to public service announcements and more than 3,000 local events, Nickelodeon went dark from noon to 3 p.m. to encourage kids to go outside and play. They also committed more than $30 million and 10 percent of its airtime to promoting health and wellness messaging.

There are reports that food companies are getting around the restrictions on television advertising by going to the Internet, where the marketing of junk food is unregulated. The

Kaiser Family Foundation contends that 85 percent of businesses advertising to children on television also had interactive websites for children promoting their branded products. In a three-month monitoring project, over 12 million children visited websites promoting food and beverage products.

Certainly, any solution to childhood obesity must include reforming the nation's sedentary lifestyle and "screen time activities" (including computers and video games). The American Academy of Pediatrics recommends that children watch no more than two hours of television or computer screens per day.

Further, experts reveal that a child's taste for protein-rich foods, like meat and fish, is inherited, but vegetables and desserts are acquired tastes that can be influenced. They encourage parents to offer a variety of vegetables and healthy foods, like fruit, for dessert. Parents are advised to focus on healthy eating and an active lifestyle rather than on a child's weight control. By eating healthy meals, children will have the energy necessary for physical activity, sports and learning.

4

Even the "Healthy" Choices at Fast-Food Restaurants Are Unhealthy

Michele Simon

Michele Simon is founder and director of the Center for Informed Food Choices and author of Appetite for Profit: How the Food Industry Undermines Our Health and How to Fight Back.

In response to sharpening criticism from nutrition advocates, fast-food franchises have added supposedly "healthy" options to their menus. For instance, McDonald's has launched a line of "premium" salads and now offers apple slices and apple juice or milk with its Happy Meals as alternatives to fries and sodas. However, these new menu items are anything but healthy. Besides being labeled with misleading dietary information, one of the worst-offending McDonald's salads has as many calories and grams of fat as a Big Mac. Also, the new Happy Meal option, which includes a sugar-loaded caramel dipping sauce, does nothing to offset the high calories and dismally low nutritional value of McDonald's hamburgers, cheeseburgers, and Chicken McNuggets. Moreover, the profits from the more-healthy fast-food options do not add up to those of the millions of burgers served every day, and so the more-healthy choices are often discontinued.

Michele Simon, "Nutriwashing Fast Food," in *Appetite for Profit: How the Food Industry Undermines Our Health and How to Fight Back.* New York: Nation Books, 2006, pp. 67–68, 71–75, 79–81, 83–84. Copyright © Michele Simon 2006. All rights reserved. Reprinted by permission of Nation Books, a member of Perseus Books Group. In the UK by permission of the author.

Let's be honest. McDonald's french fries taste good. Really good. Founder Ray Kroc didn't turn the fast-food chain into such a phenomenal success by selling lettuce. Good nutrition was about the last thing on the milkshake salesman's mind. Kroc's 1950s vision of dining has since spread to thirty thousand restaurants in 120 countries, serving fifty million customers a day and counting. That's a lot of burgers and fries. But this rapacious business model is not stopping McDonald's from trying to claim that it has the answer to America's health problems.

Years ago, the environmental movement coined the term "greenwashing" to describe how corporations use public relations [PR] to make themselves appear environmentally friendly. Today, nutrition advocates need their own moniker for a similar trend among major food companies—I like to call it "nutriwashing." As the food industry finds itself increasingly under attack for promoting unhealthy foods, one of its major defense strategies is to improve, or promise to improve, the nutritional content of its food.

McDonald's wants its customers to associate the idea of health lifestyles with its brand.

Among the major peddlers of fast food, McDonald's has borne the brunt of the criticism from nutrition advocates, many of whom are especially troubled by the company's shameless marketing to children. In response, the corporation has developed a massive PR campaign aimed at convincing us that it really does care. But before believing the spin, we should ask whether these moves have any positive impact on the nation's health, or if, worse, the campaign could actually encourage people to eat more of the wrong foods. . . .

Ulterior Motives

By the time the obesity debate started heating up, McDonald's was already a company in need of serious spin control. So, in

April 2004, with then U.S. secretary of Health and Human Services (HHS) Tommy Thompson at its side, McDonald's announced "an unprecedented, comprehensive balanced lifestyles platform to help address obesity in America and improve the nation's overall physical well-being." Sounds very impressive, until you bother to scratch the surface. The major news outlets focused largely on the initiative's "Go Active! Adult Happy Meal" component, which included a "premium salad," bottled water, and a pedometer. Other "highlights" of the plan included how McDonald's promised to take an "industry-leading role" in working with HHS to determine the best way to "communicate" nutrition information to consumers. (Are the folks who invented the Big Mac really the best candidates for this job?)

An important concept in brand marketing is the "halo effect," which is the generalization of a positive feeling about a brand from one good trait. In other words, if you think that a food company is selling healthy products, this can generate an overall good feeling about the company's brand. Whether or not the items are actually any healthier is beside the point.

Mary Dillon is responsible for McDonald's global marketing strategy and brand development, as well as the company's Balanced, Active Lifestyles initiative. Here is how Dillon describes the effort: "McDonald's cares about the well-being of each of its guests throughout the world, and by making balanced, active lifestyles an integral part of the brand we aim to make a difference in this area of their lives." In other words, McDonald's wants its customers to associate the *idea* of healthy lifestyles with its brand—a classic halo effect maneuver.

An Unhealthy Salad

In 2003, the nonprofit Physicians Committee for Responsible Medicine (PCRM) conducted a nutritional analysis of thirty-four salads served at fast-food chains, and the results, to put it mildly, were dismal. The group awarded only two menu items (from Au Bon Pain and Subway) an "outstanding" rating for being high in fiber and low in saturated fat, cholesterol, sodium, and calories. McDonald's salads were among the worst offenders. PCRM noted that all of the corporation's salad entrees contain chicken (which has virtually as much cholesterol as beef) and concluded that the salads "may very well clog up your arteries." The group also awarded the Bacon Ranch Salad with Crispy Chicken and Newman's Own Ranch Dressing "the dubious distinction of having the most fat of any salad rated. At 661 calories and 51 grams of fat, this salad is a diet disaster," with "more fat and calories and just as much cholesterol as a Big Mac."

McDonald's number-one motivation is to keep its customers addicted to its products, and lettuce covered with fried chicken furthers that goal.

Curiously, when I checked the current data on the Bacon Ranch Salad with Crispy Chicken at the company's Web site, the numbers were different. (The salad is listed at 510 calories and 31 grams of fat.) When I asked dietitian Brie Turner-McGrievy (who conducted the PCRM study) to explain the discrepancy, she said that the site numbers must have changed, since she used data that was posted in 2003. She also noted that right after her group's study was released, McDonald's changed their nutrition facts to list all of the salads without chicken as an option. (This was not available prior to the survey.) "So we know they went back to look at their nutrition facts after our review. I wouldn't be surprised if they reanalyzed their salads—maybe using less dressing or less chicken—to come up with more favorable ratings," she said.

Whatever the number of calories, merely calling something a salad doesn't make it healthy. Also, calling chicken "crispy" instead of fried is misleading. Essentially what

McDonald's has done is taken the contents of its chicken sandwiches, dumped them on top of some lettuce, and served it up with a creamy dressing. As Bob Sandelman—whose market research firm specializes in the restaurant industry—told the press, food chains "have doctored those products up. If people really knew, they would find out that the salads pack more fat and calories. That's why the key word in all this is 'perceived' to be healthy." The Fruit & Walnut Salad is better at 310 calories, but it's unlikely to hold you for a meal since it's just apples, grapes, and a few "candied walnuts," even with the "creamy low-fat yogurt."

McDonald's number-one motivation is to keep its customers addicted to its products, and lettuce covered with fried chicken furthers that goal. But touting its "premium salads" gives the false impression that the company sells healthy items.

Not Happier Meals

In response to charges that it's turning a new generation of young people into loyal Big Mac and McFlurry fans, McDonald's now offers "Happy Meal Choices." The new and improved Happy Meal gives parents the option of replacing high-fat french fries with "Apple Dippers" (sliced apples and caramel dipping sauce). Instead of a Coke, kids can now have apple juice or milk. There is, however, no substitute for the hamburger, cheeseburger, or Chicken McNuggets.

But is this any real improvement? Probably not. For a toddler who needs about 1,000 calories per day, a Happy Meal consisting of four Chicken McNuggets, small french fries, and low-fat chocolate milk totals 580 calories, or more than half of a child's daily recommended calorie intake. This of course says nothing about the dismal nutritional quality of these foods, which are devoid of fiber as well as vitamins and minerals that are especially important for growing children. And while it's true that the "Apple Dippers" in the Happy Meal contain fewer calories than french fries, this "improvement" hardly compensates for the heavy dose of sugar delivered by the dipping sauce that kids are sure to love. . . .

A Small Fraction Are Healthier

In 2005, McDonald's conceded that despite all the hoopla around its new salad offerings, only a tiny fraction of its customers actually orders them. While the company loudly trumpets the sale of 400 million premium salads since their introduction in 2003, that number is dwarfed by the total body count. McDonald's serves 23 million people a day in the United States alone, or roughly 16.8 billion people in the two-year period since the salads' introduction. As the *Washington Post* calculated, this means that in mid-2005 just 2.4 percent of McDonald's customers had ordered salads since they were added to the menu.

[Healthy menu options] make for effective window dressing, helping to keep critics and regulators quiet.

We need look no further than the fast-food king itself to confirm these stats: McDonald's spokesperson Bill Whitman explained, "The most popular item on our menu continues to be the double cheeseburger, hands down." McDonald's isn't alone in this regard. Data from NPD Foodworld indicate that the number-one entree ordered by men in America is a hamburger and the number-one selection among women is french fries, followed by hamburgers. Also, a typical Burger King outlet sells only 4 or 5 of its allegedly healthier Veggie Burgers in a day compared to 300 to 500 of any other sandwich or burger on the menu.

Burgers More Profitable

Fast-food-chains are faced with unavoidable food-related obstacles when it comes to serving truly healthy alternatives. For example, produce is much harder to store than, say, frozen hamburger patties. Other challenges include standardization and mass production of messy, perishable fruits and vegetables. Such annoyances of nature add up to more complexity and higher costs. As Matthew Paull, McDonald's chief financial officer candidly explained to the *Economist* magazine, "There is no question that we make more money from selling hamburgers and cheeseburgers."

As a result, one of the basic tenets of fast-food economics is the so-called 80-20 rule, which holds that 80 percent of a fast-food company's revenue derives from 20 percent of its products, usually its flagship line of burgers and fries. As *Forbes* magazine writer Tom Van Riper explains, so-called healthier fare at fast-food chains serves only a narrow fraction of the population while conveniently deflecting attention away from the remainder of the unwholesome menu:

> Certainly, soups and salads have added incremental revenue, since they serve that segment that has made a commitment to healthier eating. They also make for effective window dressing, helping to keep critics and regulators quiet. But a fast-food fixture that has measured its success in terms of "billions served" can't live on lightweight salads that people can get anywhere. It must beef up sales of Big Macs and Quarter Pounders. Given the 80-20 rule, a 5% drop in burger and fries sales, coupled with a 10% gain in "new menu" items, would net out to a 2% drop in revenue. For a $20 billion company like McDonald's, that's a $400 million hit. . . .

Game Over

Getting products (any products) into the mouths of cash-carrying customers is of course the top priority for food marketers. So when one of their creations fails to "show them the money," it gets swept into the dustbin of failed ideas. Such was the fate of the apparently less than popular Go Active! Adult Happy Meal, which was jettisoned by McDonald's after it had dutifully delivered the desired halo effect following the

2004 press conference. A nice McDonald's "customer satisfaction representative" apologized when I asked if it was still available, explaining that it was a "limited-time promotion." Other "well-intentioned" menu innovations have also met their untimely demises at the hands of major restaurant chains. For example, in 2004 Ruby Tuesday reduced some portion sizes and added healthier items. However, when slumping sales threatened quarterly returns, the company soon returned to its roots, aggressively promoting its biggest burgers and restoring its larger portions of french fries and pasta. Similarly, while Wendy's garnered great press in February 2005 for its "bold" decision to add fresh fruit to its menu, that resolution was rescinded as soon as corporate headquarters reviewed the disappointing sales figures a few months later. As the *Washington Post* explained in 2005, "Fast-food and casual dining chains are slowly going back to what they do best: indulging Americans' taste for high-calorie, high-fat fare."

5

Eating Healthy Foods May Be Too Expensive for the Poor

Carla Williams

Carla Williams is a writer and former contributor to the medical unit of ABC News.

According to new research published in the Journal of the American Dietetic Association, *the price of eating the daily recommended servings of healthy fruits and vegetables may be too high for low-income families. And those families are drawn to fast food not just because it is cheap; their main concern is not going to bed hungry at night, and fast food, which is high in fat and sugar, fills them up. To help low-income families eat more healthful foods, the government should make efforts to subsidize the high cost of eating, such as placing a small tax on foods with low nutritional value to lower the prices of fresh produce. Lowering food prices, however, may not be enough—the government should also sponsor educational programs to change people's attitudes about eating.*

We tend to blame the obesity epidemic in the United States on people making the wrong lifestyle choices—for example, eating a Big Mac instead of carrot sticks or Twinkles instead of an apple.

New research shows, however, that the price of healthy food may be too high for many low-income families to afford, and experts say the government needs to step in.

A new study published in the *Journal of the American Dietetic Association* finds that a low-income family would have to devote 43 to 70 percent of its food budget to fruits and vegetables to meet the 2005 Dietary Guidelines, which recommends five to nine servings of fruits and vegetables a day.

"Most Americans fall short of the recommended servings," says Milton Stokes, a registered dietitian and a spokesman for the American Dietetic Association.

"The lower their economic status, the more of their income is spent toward food," he says. "Someone making $20,000 is going to spend a larger percentage of dollars on food than someone making $200,000, even if they buy the same amount."

Currently, researchers say that American families spend 15 to 18 percent of their budget on fruits and vegetables.

"It seems unlikely that consumers would be able to increase their spending on fruits and vegetables by 200 percent to 400 percent without substantial changes elsewhere in the food budget, or from other household expenditures," the authors of the report note. "For low-income consumers this may be especially challenging, because there are few discretionary funds available in these other accounts."

If the cost of fruits and vegetables is cut in half, you are still going to have people who ... don't know how to incorporate them into their diets.

Cultural and Financial Reasons

Fruits and vegetables tend to be more expensive than processed foods for a number of reasons.

Fresh produce has a short shelf life, which means that it spoils and therefore can't be bought in bulk and stored in the same way processed or preserved foods can.

Fruits and veggies also lack the backing of government subsidies, such as those for products like high fructose corn syrup, and they can't be mass produced in an automated assembly line. We just have to wait for nature to ripen the apples.

However, reducing the price of fruits and vegetables will not necessarily cause people to eat them more often. Dr. David Katz, director of the Prevention Research Center at the Yale University School of Medicine, explains how the problem is cultural as well as financial.

"If you took the price of fruits and vegetables down by 10 percent, consumption would not increase," he says. "There are barriers that go beyond the issue of price. For example, if you pay for health insurance, it doesn't mean that health care improves.

"The same holds true with fruit consumption. If the cost of fruits and vegetables is cut in half, you are still going to have people who aren't used to eating them and who don't know how to incorporate them into their diets. Habits have to change. Reducing the financial barrier is only the first step."

And even if people are able to afford produce, a bag of carrots isn't going to fill you up the way a Snickers bar does.

"The major concern for low-income groups is not to be hungry, at night," says Adam Drewnowski, director of the Center for Obesity Research at the University of Washington in Seattle. "They gravitate to foods that fill them up—foods that are high in fat and sugar. For them, vitamins and minerals are a luxury."

Furthermore, availability can also present a problem for low-income families.

"The neighborhood you live in affects consumption because supermarkets in low-income neighborhoods may have less-appealing produce, so people are less likely to buy it, or people may shop at a bodega instead of a supermarket where produce is less available," says Katz.

Better Habits Needed

Experts say that the problem can be solved only by eliminating financial barriers, creating incentives to buy healthy foods, and cultivating changes in peoples' attitudes.

"One idea is to place a small tax on foods with low nutritional value, like soda, for example, and to use the revenue collected to subsidize fruits and vegetables," says Katz. "A tax on low nutritional foods could be the funding source to subsidize foods with a higher nutritional value."

Another solution might be to link the purchasing power of food stamps to the nutritional quality of the food.

"For example, if people are buying junk food, a $1 food stamp is worth $1 of food," Katz explains. "But that same $1 could be worth $2 if people are purchasing fruits and vegetables."

Drewnowski believes that the government needs to play a larger role in subsidizing fruits and vegetables.

Paying more for fruits and vegetables now *holds long-term savings for both families and the government in the future.*

"This problem no longer lies with individuals," he says. "There needs to be a concerted government-initiated policy to deal with the issue."

In addition to a larger governmental role, the authors believe education is necessary.

"There is a need to educate consumers about the importance of increasing their consumption of fruits and vegetables, yet these education programs must consider the tradeoffs required for families to purchase more fruits and vegetables," the authors say. "Education on household budgeting and follow-up with consumers may be needed as people work to change spending habits to eat more healthfully," they write.

In the long run, paying more for fruits and vegetables *now* holds long-term savings for both families and the government in the future. The reason experts recommend so many servings of fruits and vegetables is that they offer the best way to prevent chronic diseases such as diabetes and cancer.

"The more fruits and vegetables you include in your diet, the lower your risk for all the major chronic health problems, such as heart disease, diabetes, many cancers, high blood pressure, the list goes on," says Keith-Thomas Ayoob, associate professor of pediatrics at the Albert Einstein College of Medicine in New York.

"I think of it as spending $65 every two weeks to help prevent a family of four from getting cancer, heart disease and diabetes. That's cheap. No medication can do that so this is money that is well spent." Katz agrees.

"Both food stamps and health insurance for the poor are government subsidized programs," he says. "The government is paying people to eat poorly and then is paying to deal with the health consequences.

"It would be more economical to pay people to eat well so that you don't have to treat them in the hospital when they have heart disease and diabetes."

6

Fast-Food Franchises Are Unfairly Targeted for Serving Unhealthy Food

Greg Beato

Greg Beato is a writer and a contributing editor at Reason *magazine. He lives in San Francisco, California.*

Fast-food giants are frequently criticized for peddling fattening, artery-clogging burgers, fries, and other menu items, but long before McDonald's was franchised, lunch wagons, diners, and drive-ins offered fatty, sugary food. In fact, these independently owned restaurants dare customers to eat unhealthy meals, such as steak dinners with the caloric content of ten Big Macs and sky-high platters of burgers and fries. However, instead of being lambasted by nutritionists and anti-fast-food crusaders, these establishments are lauded for bringing communities together and serving up authentic, greasy American fare. The food at McDonald's, Wendy's, and the like pale in comparison—for which we should be thankful.

Imagine McDonald's picked up your bill any time you managed to eat 10 Big Macs in an hour or less. What if Wendy's replaced its wimpy Baconator with an unstoppable meat-based assassin that could truly make your aorta explode—say, 20 strips of bacon instead of six, enough cheese slices to roof a house, and instead of two measly half-pound patties that look as emaciated as the Olsen twins, five pounds of the finest

Greg Beato, "Where's the Beef? Thank McDonald's for Keeping You Thin," *Reason*, January 2008, pp. 15–16. Copyright © 2008 by Reason Foundation, 3415 S. Sepulveda Blvd., Suite 400, Los Angeles, CA 90034, www.reason.com. Reproduced by permission.

ground beef, with five pounds of fries on the side? [*Super Size Me* director and star] Morgan Spurlock's liver would seek immediate long-term asylum at the nearest vegan co-op.

Alas, this spectacle will never come to pass. McDonald's, Wendy's, and the rest of their fast-food brethren are far too cowed by their critics to commit such crimes against gastronomy. But you can get a free dinner with as many calories as 10 Big Macs at the Big Texan Steak Ranch in Amarillo, Texas, if you can eat a 72-ounce sirloin steak, a baked potato, a salad, a dinner roll, and a shrimp cocktail in 60 minutes or less. And if you're craving 10 pounds of junk food on a single plate, just go to Eagle's Deli in Boston, Massachusetts, where the 10-storey Challenge Burger rises so high you practically need a ladder to eat it.

A Savory Scapegoat

Fast food makes such a savory scapegoat for our perpetual girth control failures that it's easy to forget we eat less than 20 percent of our meals at the Golden Arches and its ilk. It's also easy to forget that before America fell in love with cheap, convenient, standardized junk food, it loved cheap, convenient, independently deep-fried junk food.

During the first decades of the 20th century, lunch wagons, the predecessors to diners, were so popular that cities often passed regulations limiting their hours of operation. In 1952, three years before Ray Kroc franchised his first McDonald's, one out of four American adults was considered overweight; a *New York Times* editorial declared that obesity was "our nation's primary health problem." The idea that rootless corporate invaders derailed our healthy native diet may be chicken soup for the tubby trial lawyer's soul, but in reality overeating fatty, salty, sugar-laden food is as American as apple pie.

Nowhere is this truth dramatized more deliciously than in basic-cable fare like the Food Channel's *Diners, Drive-Ins, and*

Dives and the Travel Channel's *World's Best Places to Pig Out*. Watch these shows often enough, and your Trinitron may develop Type 2 diabetes. Big Macs and BK Stackers wouldn't even pass as hors d'oeuvres at these heart attack factories.

Community Centers

Yet unlike fast food chains, which are generally characterized as sterile hegemons that force-feed us like foie gras geese, these independently owned and operated greasy spoons are touted as the very (sclerosed) heart of whatever town they're situated in, the key to the region's unique flavor, and, ultimately, the essence of that great, multicultural melting pot that puts every homogenizing fast-food fryolator to shame: America!

Instead of atomizing families and communities, dives and diners bring them together. Instead of tempting us with empty calories at cheap prices, they offer comfort food and honest value. Instead of destroying our health, they serve us greasy authenticity on platters the size of manhole covers.

As the patrons of these temples to cholesterol dig into sandwiches so big they could plug the Lincoln Tunnel, they always say the same thing. They've been coming to these places for years. They started out as kids accompanying their parents, and now they bring their kids with them.

Relative Restraint

While such scenes play out, you can't help but wonder: Doesn't that obesity lawsuit trailblazer John Banzhaf have cable? Shouldn't he be ejaculating torts out of every orifice upon witnessing such candid testimonies to the addictive power of old-timey diner fare? And more important: Shouldn't we thank our fast food chains for driving so many of these places out of business and thus limiting our exposure to chili burgers buried beneath landfills of onion rings? Were it not for the relative restraint of Big Macs and Quarter Pounders, the jiggling behemoths who bruise the scales on *The Biggest Loser* each week might instead be our best candidates for *America's Next Top Model.*

When *Super Size Me* appeared in theaters and fast food replaced [terrorist leader] Osama bin Laden as the greatest threat to the American way of life, the industry sought refuge in fruit and yogurt cups and the bland, sensible countenance of Jared the Subway Guy. Today chains are still trying to sell the idea that they offer healthy choices to their customers; see, for example, Burger King's plans to sell apple sticks dolled up in French fry drag. But they're starting to reclaim their boldness too, provoking the wrath of would-be reformers once again.

Only diet hucksters and true chowhounds would benefit from a world where the local McDonald's gave way to places serving 72-ounce steaks and [sky-high] burgers.

[In summer 2007], when McDonald's started selling supersized sodas under a wonderfully evocative pseudonym, the Hugo, it earned a prompt tsk-tsk-ing from *The New York Times.* When Hardee's unveiled its latest affront to sensible eating, a 920-calorie breakfast burrito, the senior nutritionist for the Center for Science in the Public Interest derided it as "another lousy invention by a fast-food company." When *San Francisco Chronicle* columnist Mark Morford saw a TV commercial for Wendy's Baconator, he fulminated like a calorically correct Jerry Falwell: "Have the noxious fast-food titans not yet been forced to stop concocting vile products like this, or at least to dial down the garish marketing of their most ultra-toxic products, given how the vast majority of Americans have now learned (haven't they?) at least a tiny modicum about human health?"

Forcing Accountability

Culinary reformers around the country have been trying to turn such microwaved rhetoric into reality. In New York City, health officials have been attempting to introduce a regulation that will require any restaurant that voluntarily publicizes nutritional information about its fare to post calorie counts on its menus and menu boards. Because most single-unit operations don't provide such information in any form, this requirement will apply mainly to fast-food outlets and other chains. When a federal judge ruled against the city's original ordinance, city health officials went back for seconds, revising the proposal to comply with his ruling. If this revised proposal goes into effect, any chain that operates 15 or more restaurants under the same name nationally will have to post nutritional information on the menus and menu boards of the outlets it operates in New York City. [In April 2008 this law was passed.]

In Los Angeles, City Council-member Jan Perry has been trying to get her colleagues to support an ordinance that would impose a moratorium on fast-food chains in South L.A., where 28 percent of the 700,000 residents live in poverty and 45 percent of the 900 or so restaurants serve fast food. "The people don't want them, but when they don't have any other options, they may gravitate to what's there," Perry told the *Los Angeles Times*, gravitating toward juicy, flame-broiled delusion. Apparently her constituents are choking down Big Macs only because they've already eaten all the neighborhood cats and figure that lunch at McDonald's might be slightly less painful than starving to death. And how exactly will banning fast-food outlets encourage Wolfgang Puck and Whole Foods Markets to set up shop in a part of town they've previously avoided? Is the threat of going head to head with Chicken McNuggets that much of a disincentive?

Suppose reformers like Perry get their wish and fast-food chains are regulated out of existence. Would the diners and dives we celebrate on basic cable start serving five-pound veggie burgers with five pounds of kale on the side? Only diet hucksters and true chowhounds would benefit from a world where the local McDonald's gave way to places serving 72-ounce steaks and burgers that reach toward the heavens like Manhattan skyscrapers. The rest of us would be left longing for that bygone era when, on every block, you could pick up something relatively light and healthy, like a Double Western Bacon Cheeseburger from Carl's Jr.

7

Farmworkers Are Not Being Exploited

Reginald L. Brown

Reginald L. Brown is executive vice president of the Florida To-mato Growers Exchange.

From hurricanes to increased competition from Mexico and Canada, tomato growers in the United States face numerous challenges. The accusations of worker abuse, exploitation, and enslavement on tomato farms is another one of those challenges. But in reality, tomato growers treat their workers well, providing them with clean housing and utilities for free and paying them wages that can reach more than double the minimum wage. More importantly, the penny-per-pound initiative supported by Yum! Brands, which operates Taco Bell and Pizza Hut, and McDonald's is flawed on several accounts. Through this plan, fast-food franchises are supposed to be able to directly pay to-mato pickers one extra penny for every pound of tomatoes picked. However, it is a critical fact that workers who should receive the additional payment cannot be identified. Therefore, distributing the extra wages fairly would be impossible and lead to accusa-tions of fraud and to lawsuits.

My name is Reggie Brown. I am the Executive Vice President of the Florida Tomato Growers Exchange (the Exchange). I worked for the Collier County Extension Direc-tor for the Florida Cooperative Extension Service in the 1980's. I worked for the Florida Fruit & Vegetable Association as Mar-

Reginald L. Brown, testimony before the U.S. Senate Committee on Health, Education, Labor and Pensions, April 15, 2008.

keting Director for eleven years before working for the tomato industry. Our members are tomato growers. We harvest generally from November through May. Almost half of all the tomatoes consumed in the United States year-round come from the Sunshine State.

Tomato growers have seen major challenges in recent years from hurricanes, invasive pests and diseases, and increased international competition from Mexico and Canada. The fruit and vegetable industry is a critically important sector of Florida agriculture, which is second only to tourism in importance to the state's economy. According to a 2006 University of Florida study, agriculture, food manufacturing and natural resource industries in Florida directly create more than 400,000 full- and part-time jobs, with a total employment impact of more than 700,000 full-time and part-time jobs. The direct value-added contribution is estimated at $20.32 billion, with a total impact of $41.99 billion.

During the winter, Florida competes in the U.S. marketplace with Mexico and Canada. During the six- to seven-month harvesting season, Florida's tomato growers employ more than 30,000 tomato workers.

Just as our growers need the seeds, rain and Florida sunshine, we need the workers to harvest our crops. We value the services of our workers by paying and treating our workers fairly. The fact that thousands voluntarily return to our fields to pick tomatoes year after year, decade after decade, demonstrates that fact.

False Charges

We are here before this Committee because the Coalition of Immokalee Workers (CIW), a purported Florida labor organization, has leveled accusations at Florida's tomato growers on a number of fronts. We thank you for the opportunity today to state the facts, which stand in stark contrast to the CIW's charges.

In the past several years, the CIW has organized boycotts of major fast-food corporations and demanded that these companies pay an extra penny-per-pound to workers who pick the tomatoes they buy. Two fast-food companies, Yum! Brands and McDonald's, agreed to the deal and in turn have pressured Florida's tomato growers to take on the role of passing the extra payments on to their workers. For a number of sound business and legal reasons, the producers have declined to participate.

In the meantime, the CIW also has accused Florida's tomato producers of slavery, substandard housing, abusive working conditions, and sub-poverty wages. Each claim raised—housing, wages, working conditions, and slavery—[is] addressed by local, State and Federal laws. We absolutely agree with the Committee that these laws should be aggressively enforced. Our growers comply with all of these laws and many others, too.

We have asked for any evidence that would substantiate these allegations [of slavery] against growers of Florida tomatoes and have received none.

My testimony today will refute the false allegations that have been made by the CIW and perpetuated in the media. It also will outline the growers' concerns over the penny-per-pound initiative, explain the technical and legal reasons they have chosen not to participate and suggest better solutions to improve the lives of farm workers.

Slavery Not an Issue

First, let me state unequivocally that Florida's tomato growers abhor and condemn slavery. We are on the same side on this issue. It is outrageous to have slavery happening in Florida or in any other state. However, charges that tomato growers have enslaved workers are false and defamatory. Indeed, in correspondence with Members of this Committee and during meetings with Senators and staff, we have denounced slavery and these unsubstantiated claims. We could not survive without our valued employees.

On numerous occasions, we have asked for any evidence that would substantiate these allegations against growers of Florida tomatoes and have received none. To the best of our knowledge, CIW has not taken any such evidence to the appropriate federal, state or local authorities who are vested with oversight in these matters. If we had any information indicating a grower was involved in slavery, we would immediately turn it over to authorities and assist in prosecution.

There is some confusion involving labor contractors and their relationship with growers. Like the workers, these contractors are employed by the growers. They assemble a crew and bring them to a farm and they, as well as the workers, are paid directly by the grower. To ensure that the workers are treated fairly and paid directly, growers participate in the SAFE [Socially Accountable Farm Employers] program described in greater detail below. SAFE provides certification by an independent third party that the working conditions are safe and fair for the workers. No other produce group in the country has such a program to help workers.

Like all Americans, we are angered that slavery is even an issue in America in 2008. The reality, however, is that there are indeed cases of slavery and human trafficking occurring in many states today, and that is a tragedy.

Existing Worker Benefits

Many of our growers provide free or inexpensive housing that must pass government inspection. Many employers also pay for utilities, including gas, electric, water and garbage, even when workers are not picking tomatoes. We are committed to provide positive housing solutions for our workers and their families.

We are not aware of any substandard housing being owned, operated or controlled by any member of our Exchange. I was advised by Members of this Committee of substandard housing in Immokalee, Florida. We requested any specific information that might help us investigate but received none. However, we did contact the Collier County Commissioner for Immokalee and asked that appropriate county agencies query the CIW about any specific cases of substandard housing, follow-up on the complaint and enforce the County's housing code.

Broad charges have been made that workers are being exploited and that Florida tomato growers are not following labor standards. We firmly deny these allegations. Again, we have asked for specific information on where this might be occurring so we could notify the proper authorities. We received no response, nor do we have any other information about worker standards violations.

Tomato harvesters' wages potentially can exceed, by a considerable margin, the hourly wage for most workers at fast-food restaurants.

It is difficult to prove a negative—that our members are not and have no pattern of exploiting our workers. However, we believe we can in this case offer clear evidence of commitment to providing all of our workers a safe, secure working environment that complies with all laws and standards of performance.

In 2005, we met with officials from McDonald's to discuss how our growers could best show we were improving working conditions for our workers. Based on these discussions with McDonald's and others in the industry, a program was developed that calls for thorough, direct auditing by an independent third party to assure that working standards are met and that workers are receiving the wages to which they are entitled. This program is the first of its kind in the U.S. produce industry. Indeed, McDonald's web site indicates as part of its social responsibility program that it collaborated with us "to improve conditions for farm workers in the Florida tomato industry."

The program is Socially Accountable Farm Employers, or SAFE. SAFE is an independent, nonprofit organization that independently audits and certifies fair, legal farm labor practices in the agriculture industry. It is a serious program that addresses important issues such as working conditions and wages. SAFE's certification signifies that a grower has complied with all employment laws and regulations such as the Migrant and Seasonal Worker Protection Act, and that the grower fosters a work environment that is free of hazard, intimidation, violence and harassment.

Fair Wages Bring Workers Back

Exchange members pay their employees competitive wages. We must, if we are to have workers each season to plant and harvest the crops. Otherwise, workers will go elsewhere. Yet each year thousands of workers return to the region to harvest Florida's tomatoes.

It's important to note that farm workers are seasonal employees who often work for multiple employers during the year, so what a worker might earn on a farm in Immokalee constitutes only part of his or her wages for the whole year.

Tomato harvesters have the opportunity to earn more than double the federal minimum wage of $5.85 and nearly double Florida's $6.79 per hour. These are legal, competitive and fair wages. Not only has the minimum wage increased in the past 20 years, the per-bucket rate workers earn has gone up as well. Yes, sometimes workers' hours are cut short because the weather is bad and they can't pick the tomatoes, or there are no tomatoes to be picked. Yet tomato harvesters' wages potentially can exceed, by a considerable margin, the hourly wage for most workers at fast-food restaurants.

In addition, the growers comply with all withholding of taxes and payment of FUTA [Federal Unemployment Tax Act], SUTA [State Unemployment Tax Authority] and WC [workers' compensation] contributions according to law.

Based on payroll records our members submitted to the federal government for the last growing season, the average rate was between $10.50 and $14.86 per hour for tomato harvesters. We believe it may be higher for the 2007–2008 crop year. Again, these wages will be just a portion of the annual income for harvesters who move on to other crops in other regions.

Penny-per-Pound Program

Our Exchange is a voluntary association of tomato growers. As a group, the growers have made a business decision not to participate in the penny-per-pound distribution arrangement, as is their right. My goal today is to explain as clearly as possible the reasons behind that decision.

Because the Exchange's members have not seen the agreements announced by Yum! Brands and McDonald's and don't know the specific details, it is difficult to fully assess the responsibilities, liabilities and impact of CIW's program. However, from a legal standpoint, we have been advised that the potential risks of participating in the penny-per-pound agreement far outweigh any benefit.

At first blush, the penny-per-pound initiative sounds like a positive program. Fast-food chains agree to pay an extra penny for each pound of tomatoes they buy from Florida producers, with that extra penny distributed to the workers who picked them. Ostensibly, the growers would serve as the conduit through which the harvesters would receive the extra payment. But practically—and legally—speaking, the program is flawed.

For the record, we do not object to the fast-food chains paying extra to the workers who pick the tomatoes they buy. Our members simply do not want to be part of that arrangement.

However, we don't believe it is possible to legally and fairly get the extra payments into the hands of the specific harvesters who pick the tomatoes bought by the restaurants. The root of the problem is this: How can the fast-food chains (or any other company that agrees to the extra penny) accurately identify how many tomatoes come from which producer and which specific employees picked them? It is not possible, so how can they ensure the workers who picked their tomatoes are the ones who receive the additional wages?

A review of the supply chain shows why the Yum! Brands and McDonald's agreements are unworkable.

During harvest, tomatoes that the workers pick are not individually identified or labeled by worker or by customer. At the time of harvest, a tomato picked by a worker could ultimately be purchased by any number of the producer's customers.

Tomatoes are not made available for commercial channels until after they have been washed, graded to federal standards, sized and packed into cartons in a state and federally licensed packing facility. Some tomatoes (on average 20–25 percent) are never purchased because they are "dumped" for failing to meet grade or size standards, or have damage that makes them unfit for sale.

If the extra-penny funds are distributed among all of the workers, . . . some will be paid too much and others won't get what is due them.

Producers send their harvested and packed tomatoes to their customers, the repacking and distribution companies that supply the fast-food chains. A repacking facility receives tomatoes from any number of producers, and those tomatoes are then co-mingled in large lots.

An Impractical Program

We believe the suppliers have agreed to participate in the program at the insistence of the fast-food chains. McDonald's indicates on its web site that, "[o]ur suppliers will establish a way for the additional penny per pound to be given to the farmworkers." Thus, these extra-penny agreements are made among several parties: the CIW, the fast-food chains, and their suppliers.

The critical fact is that no one can identify which worker should receive an additional payment, nor can the correct payment be calculated. And if the extra-penny funds are distributed among all of the workers, the fact is some will be paid too much and others won't get what is due them. This is neither right nor fair.

We believe that education, improved housing, fair wages and safe working conditions are . . . solutions to improving the lives of farm workers and their families.

Additionally, because the extra payments are considered wages, how will the fast-food chains withhold appropriate amounts? How will they pay the required employer contributions for FUTA, SUTA and WC, which can amount to 15 to 20 percent of the wages paid?

The Exchange strongly believes that, because the parties to the agreements know it is impossible to distribute the correct payment amounts to the right workers, the growers' participation would open them up to lawsuits from workers who were knowingly treated unfairly. Workers also could allege that there is/was a scheme to defraud them, and each check issued (allegedly in an incorrect amount) could be a separate bank or wire fraud. This is by definition a RICO [Racketeer-

Influenced and Corrupt Organizations Act] case. What's more, RICO allows plaintiffs to bring additional grounds to allege fraud-based activities on whatever size "enterprise" they seek to attack. . . .

We believe if our growers participate they will be placed at a competitive disadvantage in the marketplace. We believe that ultimately fast-food chains and other companies will buy tomatoes elsewhere—most likely Mexico—because the extra penny makes Florida tomatoes more expensive. If that business shifts offshore, not only will tomato harvesters be without the extra penny, they will be without jobs. The tomato industry will go away, and Florida's economy will suffer. . . .

A Practical Improvement Plan

We call upon CIW to take on the task of providing a way for Yum! Brands and McDonald's to distribute monies to its members and workers without involving the growers. CIW, as a representative of its members and workers, should gladly accept the challenge of getting this job done. If it had figured a way to do this, its member and workers would have been receiving checks from McDonald's since November [2007]. Alternatively, like our growers do, McDonald's could contribute to charities that are helpful to CIW's members and workers, and their communities such as Catholic Charities, the University of South Florida Migrant Scholarships, the Redlands Christian Migrant Association and others.

There is no question that harvesting tomatoes is physically demanding work that most people do not want to do. Florida's tomato producers are grateful to have a steady workforce that allows us to provide Americans with a bountiful, nutritious and healthful crop.

We believe that education, improved housing, fair wages and safe working conditions are comprehensive, impactful and long-term solutions to improving the lives of farm workers and their families. We are working toward those goals and invite others to join us.

We have and continue to work with organizations such as Redlands Christian Migrant Association, Catholic Charities, University of South Florida Migrant Scholarships and others so that we can jointly create, develop and execute meaningful programs relating to health care, child care, housing and education so that farm workers and their families have a real chance to achieve the American Dream.

8

The Fast-Food Industry Contributes to the Abuse of Animals

Tina Volpe

Tina Volpe is an animal rights activist, an advocate of vegetarianism, and the author of The Fast Food Craze: Wreaking Havoc on Our Bodies and Our Animals.

Burger patties, buffalo wings, chicken nuggets, milk, and cheese that are served every day at fast-food restaurants are the products of factory-farm cruelty. Mass numbers of chickens, pigs, and cows are deprived of the basic needs of life—sunlight, fresh air, and even space to move—and are forced to live in overcrowded, filthy, and disease-ridden cages and pens. To keep from pecking each other, chickens are de-beaked using a painful procedure, while others are scalded alive. Cattle that are supposed to be "stunned" before slaughter are often hung upside down, stabbed, or boiled while still fully conscious, struggling and feeling pain. And dairy cows are chained in concrete-floored sheds, repeatedly impregnated to keep producing milk—putting great strains on their bodies—and pumped up with synthetic diets that result in infection and disease.

My sister told me a story the other day about an acquaintance of hers who mentioned her husband was away on a hunting trip. The woman stated she would never eat the meat of the animal he shot and brought home . . . she couldn't endure eating a creature as cute as a deer . . . although, that very same day, she took her kids to McDonald's for hamburgers. Where did she think the meat came from that went into the meal her family consumed? It simply amazed me how little awareness was involved in this scenario. Do most people think that the burgers and nuggets that come from these fast food places, stores and restaurants actually just come from a scientist's lab or from the ground?. . .

[The] deer that was shot in the forest (and I disagree with killing any animals) did suffer and die; however, there is no degree of suffering comparable to that of a factory-farmed animal—those same animals that get pushed into greasy burger patties, buffalo wings, chicken nuggets, eggs, milk, cheese, and every dairy product. These animals never knew what life was like in nature, never felt the dirt under their feet or felt the sunshine on their bodies, even just the simple, common everyday blessings that we take for granted, that God intended for them and gave them the right to enjoy. . . . Bless their little hearts for what they went through to feed most of America and what they go through every second of every minute of every hour of every day. . . .

Chickens in Factory Farms

Now let's talk about what these creatures endure on a daily basis, for their entire lives.

In egg farms, the male chickens aren't needed so what happens to them? As soon as they poke their little precious heads out of their shells, they are swooped up and thrown into a large plastic trash bag to suffocate among their brothers. And their lives are actually better than the ones who survive.

With the growing number of humans trying to limit their intake of red meat, the poultry industries are booming. Record numbers of chickens and turkeys are being raised and killed for meat in the U.S. every year. Nearly 10 billion chickens and

0.5 billion turkeys are hatched in one year, Chickens are social and need to have some sort of pecking order to survive. Their brains are not only trained for finding food and water, there is a lot more that goes on in their instinctive lives.

> *Confined in unsanitary, disease-ridden factory farms, . . . [chickens] succumb to heat prostration, infectious diseases, and cancer.*

In factory farms these chickens have no natural sunlight, and have lost the opportunity to live their lives as nature intended. Because of this, they are literally driven insane. They peck at each other, scream, and sometimes are driven so insane, they resort to cannibalism. Chickens who are overcrowded and who are driven insane by this . . . tend to panic and jump on top of one another, killing the chickens below by smothering them. The farmers have also remedied this situation. They have decided that if they crowded the birds even more tightly, they would not be able to jump on top of each other and kill more profits. They are living in such crowded circumstances that just getting to the scientific food fed them and the water, is nearly impossible. Some of the weaker birds never make it to the food and water and end up dying of starvation and dehydration.

Horrible Solutions

The people who run these factory farms have remedied the pecking situation too! It's called de-beaking. This procedure is probably the most painful thing that can be done to a chicken. Between the horn and the bone is a thin layer of highly sensitive soft tissue resembling the quick of the human nail. The hot knife used in de-beaking cuts through this complex of horn and sensitive tissue, causing severe pain. This is done without any anesthesia or painkillers, they cut off the most sensitive part of the chickens, their beaks, so that when they do go insane and start pecking and screaming, they won't do much damage to the others. It's all about profits, you know.

Today's broiler chickens (meat) have been genetically altered to grow twice as fast and twice as large as their ancestors. In this process, hundreds of millions of chickens die every year before even reaching slaughter. They grow so fast that the heart and lungs are not developed and the results are congestive heart failure and tremendous death losses. They also experience crippling leg disorders due to abnormally heavy bodies. Confined in unsanitary, disease-ridden factory farms, the birds also succumb to heat prostration, infectious diseases, and cancer.

Chickens and turkeys are taken to the slaughterhouse in crates stacked on the backs of open trucks. When they arrive from their factory farm life (hell), they are either pulled from their crates or dumped onto a conveyor belt. Some miss the belt and die an even more grim death. Some die from being crushed by machinery, or others may die of starvation or exposure days, or even weeks later. Birds inside the slaughterhouse suffer an equally gruesome fate. They are fully conscious and hung by their feet by metal shackles on a moving rail. Chickens are excluded from the federal Humane Slaughter Act, which requires stunning prior to slaughter ... Many are placed in electrified water baths to immobilize them to hurry assembly-line killing. This procedure is even crueler because of concerns that too much electricity would damage the carcass, so they usually remain conscious and are still capable of feeling pain and fear. After the shackled birds pass through the stunning tank, their throats are slashed, usually by a mechanical blade. Inevitably the blade misses some birds, who may still be struggling and moving. The next thing that happens is the scalding tank. The ones that weren't fortunate enough to have the blade hit them are literally scalded alive. This occurs so often that the industry has a term for them. They call them "redskins." ...

Treatment of Pigs

The corporate hog factories have taken over the traditional hog farms and pigs raised for food are being treated as lifeless tools of production, rather than as living, feeling animals.

Approximately 100 million pigs are raised and slaughtered in the U.S. every year. As babies, they are subjected to painful mutilations without anesthesia or pain relievers. Their tails are cut off to minimize tail biting, something that happens when these highly intelligent animals are kept in deprived factory farm conditions. In addition, notches are taken out of the piglet's ears for identification. By two to three weeks of age, 15% of the piglets have died. Those who do [survive], are taken away from their mothers and crowded into pens with metal bars and concrete floors. A headline from *National Hog Farmer* magazine says "Crowding Pigs Pays . . ." and this is shown by the intense overcrowding in every stage of a pigs confinement system. Pigs live this way, packed into giant, warehouse-like sheds, until they reach a slaughter weight of 250 pounds at six months old.

In addition to overcrowded housing, sows and pigs also endure extreme crowding in transportation to slaughter, resulting in rampant suffering and death.

The air in hog factories is laden with dust, dander and noxious gases, which are produced as the animals' urine and feces builds up inside the sheds. For pigs, which spend their entire lives in these conditions, respiratory disease is rampant. Many other diseases are reported that are horribly painful and inhumane. Modern breeding sows are treated like piglet-making machines . . . living a continuous cycle of breeding and birth. Each sow has more than twenty piglets a year. When pregnant, the sows are confined in gestation crates—small metal pens just two feet wide to prevent them from turning around or even lying down comfortably. At the end of their four-month pregnancies, they are transferred to similar cramped crates to give birth. With barely enough room to stand up and lie down, and no bedding to speak of, many suffer from sores on their shoulders and knees. When asked about this, one pork industry representative wrote ". . . straw is very expensive and there certainly would not be a supply of straw in the country to supply all of the birthing pens in the U.S."

The psychological damage this does to pigs is unbelievable. After the sows give birth and nurse their young for two to three weeks, the piglets are taken away to be fattened and the sows are re-impregnated.

In addition to overcrowded housing, sows and pigs also endure extreme crowding in transportation to slaughter, resulting in rampant suffering and death.

Ranchers still identify cattle the same way they have since pioneer days—with hot iron brands.

Prior to being hung upside down by their back legs and bled to death at the slaughterhouse, pigs are supposed to be "stunned" and rendered unconscious, in accordance with the federal Humane Slaughter Act. However, stunning at slaughterhouses is terribly inexact, and often conscious animals are hung upside down, kicking and struggling, while a slaughterhouse worker tries to "stick" them in the neck with a knife. If the worker is unsuccessful, the pig will be carried (still kicking and struggling) to the next station . . . the scalding tank . . . where he/she will be boiled, alive and fully conscious. . . .

Cows Have Rough Lives

Many beef cattle are born and live on the range, foraging and fending for themselves for months or even years. They are not adequately protected against inclement weather and may die of dehydration or freeze to death.

Accustomed to roaming unbothered and relaxed, range cattle are frightened and confused when humans come to round them up. Terrified animals are often injured, some so severely that they become "downed" (unable to walk or even stand). These downed animals suffer for days without receiving food, water, or veterinary care, and many die of neglect. Others are dragged, beaten, and pushed with tractors on their way to slaughter. Many cattle will experience more transportation and handling stress at stockyards and auctions, where they are pushed through a series of walkways and holding pens and sold to the highest bidder.

Ranchers still identify cattle the same way they have since pioneer days—with hot iron brands. Needless to say, this practice is extremely traumatic and painful, and the animals bellow loudly as rancher's brands are burned into their skin. Beef cattle are also subjected to "[wattling]," another type of identification marking. This painful procedure entails cutting chunks out of the hide that hangs under the animals' necks. [Wattling] marks are supposed to be large enough so that ranchers can identify their cattle from a distance.

Most beef cattle spend the last few months of their lives at feed lots, crowded by the thousands into dusty, manure-laden holding pens. The air is thick with harmful bacteria and particulate matter, and the animals are at constant risk for respiratory disease. Feed lot cattle are routinely implanted with growth-promoting hormones, and they are fed unnaturally rich diets designed to fatten them up quickly and profitably. Because cattle are biologically suited to eat a grass-based, high fiber diet, their concentrated feed lot rations contribute to metabolic disorders. . . .

A standard beef slaughterhouse kills 250 cattle every hour. The high speed of the assembly line makes it increasingly difficult to provide animals with any resemblance of humane treatment. A *Meat & Poultry* article states: "Good handling is extremely difficult if equipment is 'maxed out' all the time. It is impossible to have a good attitude toward cattle if employees have to constantly overexert themselves, and thus transfer all that stress right down to the animal, just to keep up with the line." . . .

With genetic manipulation and intensive production technology, it is common for a cow to produce one hundred pounds of milk per day.

The U.S. Department of Agriculture oversees the treatment of animals in meat plants, but enforcement of the law varies dramatically. While a few plants have been forced to halt production for a few hours because of alleged animal cruelty, such sanctions are rare. . . .

Unnatural Conditions

On a typical dairy farm, cows stand on concrete, chained by the neck, in huge sheds and are milked by machines. To boost production, some farmers inject cows with synthetic growth hormones, which increase the cows' risk of developing mastitis, a painful condition that causes cows' udders to become so heavy that they sometimes drag on the ground. . . .

Regardless of where they live, all dairy cows must give birth in order to begin producing milk. Today, dairy cows are forced to birth a calf every year. Like human beings, cows have a nine-month gestation period, and so giving birth every twelve months is physically demanding. The cows are also artificially re-impregnated while they are still producing milk, so their bodies are still producing milk during seven months of their nine-month pregnancy. With genetic manipulation and intensive production technology, it is common for a cow to produce one hundred pounds of milk per day—ten times more than they would produce naturally. As a result, the cow's bodies are under constant stress and they are at risk for numerous health problems. . . .

In a healthy environment, cows would live in excess of twenty-five years, but on modern dairies, they are slaughtered and made into ground beef after just three to four years. The abuse wreaked upon the bodies of dairy cows is so intense that the dairy industry also [i]s a huge source of "downed animals."

Even though the dairy industry is familiar with the cow's health problems and suffering because of intensive milk production, it continues to subject cows to even worse abuses in the name of increased profit. Bovine Growth Hormone (BGH), a synthetic hormone, is now being injected into cows to get them to produce even more milk. Besides adversely affecting the cows' health, BGH also increases birth defects in their calves.

Calves born to dairy cows are separated from their mothers immediately after birth. The half that are born female are raised to replace older dairy cows in the milking herd. The male half are raised and slaughtered for meat. Most are killed for beef, but about one million are used for veal.

9

The Fast-Food Industry Takes Measures to Treat Animals More Humanely

Lindsey Kurach and Jessica Lynch

Lindsay Kurach and Jessica Lynch are both graduates of the University of Alberta's Department of Agricultural, Life and Environmental Sciences in Canada.

Allegations of animal abuse and consumer demand for the protection of animal welfare have led meat and egg suppliers of fast-food franchises to improve their operations and make their facilities more humane. In fact, after McDonald's created their own animal welfare policies, its biggest rivals followed suit in order to remain competitive. Today, these companies pay premium prices for humanely-raised and produced meat and eggs, which has resulted in higher-quality meat and egg production. Animal welfare experts have also taken notice and have applauded fast-food franchises and their suppliers for dramatically bettering the living conditions and slaughtering and processing standards of livestock throughout the industry.

If you asked children their favorite food, most would probably say a kid's meal from a fast food restaurant would top the list. In a society where time has become a highly valued commodity, people are often looking for fast and relatively inexpensive places to eat. [In 2004] alone, there was a 2.3 percent increase in the amount of food purchased from fast food

Lindsey Kurach and Jessica Lynch, "Humane Hamburgers: How Much Do Fast Food Restaurants Care About the Animals They Serve?" *There's a Heifer in Your Tank,* Fall 2005. pp. 2–3. Reproduced by permission.

restaurants in Canada. Recently, there has been an increase in public concern regarding how animals are treated. Some consumers are demanding that animal welfare standards be set and met by producers for the products they are purchasing, especially from fast food establishments.

A Key Lawsuit

Animal welfare concerns in the fast food industry first gained the public spotlight during the longest public relations trial in the UK's history. Helen Steel and David Morris, two London Greenpeace activists, were sued by McDonald's for distributing pamphlets to consumers that were critical of the corporation. The trial lasted just over two years, ending when the judge ruled in favor of McDonald's. However, he did highly criticize McDonald's and stated that they were ". . . culpably responsible for cruel practices in the rearing and slaughter of some of the animals which are used to produce their food." Consumers began to question animal welfare standards in the fast food industry, and soon demanded that changes be made.

McDonald's image suffered a major blow after the trial, so the company quickly responded to consumer demands. An animal welfare council, composed of six animal welfare experts, was hired, including the well-known animal behaviourist Dr. Temple Grandin. Since 1999, all beef, pork, chicken, and egg suppliers must be audited and adhere to set standards of animal welfare. In 2002 there were 500 audits conducted at processing facilities around the world. The standards of housing, handling, and humane slaughtering are all evaluated, and suppliers who do not meet standards will no longer be able to sell their product to these fast food restaurants. While most suppliers pass the audits, those that do not are given 30 days to make the necessary changes to reach McDonald's standards.

Humane Standards

Soon after McDonald's made their own policies on animal welfare, its biggest competitors followed suit. Similar animal welfare councils have been formed by hiring numerous agricultural researchers and animal behaviourists to develop humane standards and review the effectiveness of changes made by suppliers. Performing standardized audits on their suppliers has become the norm. These audits follow the guidelines developed by Dr. Grandin, who has now also been hired as a consultant for both Wendy's and Burger King. There have even been talks between companies to set industry-wide standards, likely through a third party system. "The leadership that has been shown in the past several years by fast food restaurants with respect to standards for animal care has been remarkable," says Dr. Craig Wilkinson, DVM [Doctor of Veterinary Medicine] and director of animal care for the Faculty of Agriculture, Forestry and Home Economics at the University of Alberta.

Better Quality Food

With dramatic changes in industry standards, suppliers have been forced to adopt their policies, raising questions about the costs. New housing and slaughter equipment does not come cheap. However, these investments are easily made up by increasing profits. Companies are paying more than ever for meat and eggs from humane suppliers. Research has also shown humane treatment of animals decreases injury/bruising and mortality while improving meat quality and egg production. Susan Church, the general manager of Alberta Farm Animal Care (AFAC) agrees, as she has seen that "raising the standards, regarding animal welfare, has led to better quality products." An increase in supply with better product quality leads to greater profits, which is enough reason in itself to treat animals humanely.

Enforcing standards has made a huge impact on animal welfare across North America. In 1996, audits were performed by Dr. Grandin and the USDA [U.S. Department of Agriculture], and only 30% of beef plants were in compliance with the American Meat Institute's guidelines for stunning animals. Just 4 years later, after McDonald's became involved, this number skyrocketed to 74%, and continues to climb to this day. Dr. Grandin has stated, "I have been working in the meat industry for more than 25 years and I saw more improvements in 1999 than I have seen in my entire career." Consumers demanded standards, and fast food restaurants responded above and beyond expectations. This movement may very well be the first step towards improving standards for livestock from all suppliers, making our next hamburger meal a little easier to swallow.

10

Fast-Food Culture Has Harmed Society

Joyce Marcel

Joyce Marcel is a writer and a columnist for the American Reporter *and CommonDreams.org. She lives in Vermont.*

McDonald's and other fast-food franchises stand against the values of American society: individualism, originality, creativity, nonconformity, and fearlessness. These restaurants have ushered widespread standardization and profit-maximization that have transformed American dining into a tasteless, unhealthy, prepackaged experience that is disconnected from the natural world and immersed in advertising and commercialism. Along with creating a false sense of abundance with its seemingly endless supplies of condiments, McDonald's also creates a false sense of choice with its meaningless menu. Because Americans have accepted a corruption of their food, they have come to accept corruption in every other facet of society, from health care to taxes.

McDonald's is under attack these days, but for all the wrong reasons. Yes, the fast food industry sells unhealthy food. Yes, it induces people to overeat for profit. Yes, ranchers cut down rain forests to supply it with cattle. Yes, that reduces the world's oxygen supply. But the real crime of McDonald's—supposedly the shining symbol of American capitalism—is that it is truly and deeply anti-American.

Joyce Marcel, "Fast Food Fascism," *Common Dreams*, January 23, 2003. Reproduced by permission of the author.

The fast food industry stands against the personal values that made this country great: rugged individualism, originality, creativity, a sense of adventure, non-conformity, and above all, all-around fearlessness.

In an effort to standardize products and maximize profits, the fast food industry has infected America with an insidious creeping fascism that was never political in itself, but which has had deeply political consequences.

Sit in a McDonald's for a half hour with a critical eye. The lights are glaring; there's no relaxation or goodwill to go along with the food. The chairs and tables are bolted to the ground. You can't draw up a chair to another table, for example, or join a larger group. Even if you're uncomfortably close to the table, there is nothing you can do except accept the discomfort. It's like a prison cafeteria; shut up and eat.

The foliage, furniture, plates, utensils and cups are plastic. You are completely disconnected from the natural world. All the decoration is advertisement. It's no wonder so many people wear corporate logos on their clothes and think it's right to put advertisements in schools; they're completely desensitized; life doesn't exist outside of commercials.

A False Sense

Fast food restaurants create a false sense of abundance. They offer access to a ready supply of condiments, sugar packets, straws, napkins and coffee cream—things that cost the restaurant almost nothing and have no real value.

They also offer a false sense of control. You appear to have many choices—a Big Mac, a cheeseburger, a quarter pounder, a double quarter pounder or a "Big 'n' Tasty"—but they're all pre-packaged, frozen, pre-cooked hamburger. If you want to be radical, have fried chicken, fried fish pieces, even flatbread sandwiches. But you have no control over portion size, or the way your meal is cooked.

One of the ways we learn who we are is by the choices we make. Being given free reign to make meaningless choices translates directly into the political arena, where we are asked to make empty choices between multi-millionaires and the almost identical political parties which own them.

The overworked and over-managed young food zombies in fast food restaurants are being trained to accept a lifetime of deadening and unfulfilling jobs. They learn early that making suggestions and demands will get you fired. Fear plays a large part in this kind of work; I once took out a notebook in McDonald's and the young manager looked panic-stricken. He was probably afraid of his own managers.

In order to navigate the world intelligently, we need our language to be clear and well-grounded. McDonald's corrupts language. What on earth is a "McSalad"? A "Happy Meal?" A "Mighty Kids Meal?"

Many books have been written about the frighteningly poor quality of fast food. Eric Schlosser's "Fast Food Nation: The Dark Side of the All-American Meal" is a revelation. A new book by Greg Critser, "Fat Land: How Americans Became the Fattest People in the World," reveals how the fast food industry discovered that Americans are so ashamed of appearing gluttonous that they won't order two orders of fries. In response, the industry created "supersized" portions and along with it, a nation of supersized people.

Today there are thousands of fast food restaurants and millions of people who actually believe this is the way food should be.

Degraded Standards

Once you have accepted standardization in fast food restaurants, you may be unquestioning about it in other places. In my supermarket, all the pork is now pre-packaged by a company called Smithfield. The packaging offers a list of ingredients: pork broth, potassium lactate, salt, sodium phosphates, and natural flavorings; shouldn't the only ingredient in a pork roast be pork?

The fast food industry is now under attack from many sides. McDonald's stock has lost half its market value [between 2001 and 2003]; it has closed more than 100 restaurants and fired its CEO [chief executive officer]. Its arch enemy, Burger King, was on the market for two years without finding a taker; it sold at a discounted price that dropped from $2.3 billion to $1.5 billion in just six months.

Obese people are suing fast food restaurants here, while abroad, they are being attack[ed] for corporate imperialism. McDonald's, with 23,000 restaurants in about 121 countries, has been attacked in China, Denmark, France, Bangalore, Colombia, Russia, Argentina, Belgium, South Africa and Great Britain.

My own private rebellion against fast food restaurants dates back 30 years, as I watched juicy fresh hamburgers and fried chicken disappear all across the country, along with the small, quirky family-owned restaurants that served them.

Why, I wondered, as Americans grew wealthier, did they also grow so timid? Why did they reject the adventure of discovery, of making choices, of exploring the world? Why were they willing to sacrifice flavor, freshness, variety and a strong connection to the natural world for safe, predictable, boring and homogenized food? I can't blame the fast food industry for being so eager to oblige them.

I may be leaving myself open to a charge of elitism here, but no, I don't want to become a vegetarian, and no, I don't think that wanting restaurants to serve the kind of fresh, tasty, wholesome and inexpensive food that I remember from my childhood makes me a snob.

By unquestionably accepting the corruption of their food, Americans have come to accept the corruption of just about everything else—low pay, out-of-reach health care, corporate corruption, irrational wars, tax breaks for the rich, and McPresidents of the United States.

Today there are thousands of fast food restaurants and millions of people who actually believe this is the way food should be. Is it such a great step to thinking that Americans will also accept a degraded form of something as complex, difficult and demanding as real democracy?

11

Fast-Food Culture Has Benefited Society

William H. Marling

William H. Marling is a professor in the Department of English at Case Western Reserve University in Cleveland, Ohio. He is the author of How "American" Is Globalization?

Critics claim that McDonald's is altering what and how people around the globe eat, amounting to the "McDonaldization" of the world—the infiltration of fast-food principles such as the homogenization of culture and standardization of taste. Yet, these critics offer little in the way of facts and statistics to support their arguments. Fast food, for instance, is not a uniquely American invention, nor is the "efficiency" of McDonald's service changing the already-speedy eating habits of the Japanese, Mexicans, or other nationals. Furthermore, McDonald's and its imitators do not undermine local cultures; conversely, from Beijing to Vienna, locally owned franchises adapt to the local customs and tastes and use locally produced goods. And the standards that McDonald's and others are spreading, which come in the forms of clean bathrooms, handicapped access, nondiscrimination, and charitable giving, represent values we might wish to see more of abroad.

Is the world suffering from "McDonaldization"? Critics offer no statistics, no studies, and few facts to back their generalizations. Write [globalization critics] George Ritzer and Eliza-

William H. Marling, *How "American" Is Globalization?* Baltimore: Johns Hopkins University Press, 2006, pp. 51–59. © 2006 The Johns Hopkins University Press. Reprinted with permission of The Johns Hopkins University Press.

beth L. Malone, "The most notable and more directly visible cultural impact is the way McDonald's is altering the manner in which much of the rest of the world eats. What and how people eat is a crucial component of almost all, if not all, cultures, but with the spread of the principles of McDonaldization virtually *everyone* in McDonaldized society is devouring French fries (and virtually every other kind of food) and doing so quickly, often on the run." I am not arguing for junk food here, but I do think overseas fast-food emporia deserve objective study and analysis. The known facts would suggest that McDonald's is at least as representative of *modernity* as of Americanism, and that the former rather than the latter is responsible for changes in traditional eating habits.

McDonald's opened its first foreign franchises in the 1960s, and it was soon followed by its competitors. The perception of a rise in "McDonaldization" owes much to a concurrent increase in American tourism, beginning with the 1960s backpackers. Even today, if we venture somewhere that Westerners don't go—Greenland, Nigeria, New Guinea—we find few McDonald's. But "McDonaldization" has become the rallying cry of a wide variety of modernity's foes. Food franchises are undeniably a feature of modernity and globalization, but how "American" are they?

It takes only a minute's reflection to realize that *every society has always had a form of fast food.* On Bali, one pot of food was traditionally cooked in the morning, and everyone snacked from it all day: a fast meal was rice and meat carried away on a palm leaf. In France open shop fronts have sold *crêpes*, sandwiches, and *croque-messieurs* at least since the 1940s. Today *kebab* stands dot every French town, offering carry-away meals. Germans and Austrians can buy chestnuts and *kartoffeln* from street-corner vendors if they need to eat on the run. Mexico is overrun with street-corner taco and burrito vendors. In Japan most people eat boxed meals of rice, vegetables, and a protein called *bento* for lunch. *Okonomiaki* and *takoyaki* carts still punctuate some street corners, while *soba, udon,* and *ramen*—once sold by itinerant street vendors—are everywhere available in storefronts. *Sushi* was originally fast food, sold from pushcarts, and there are now robots that turn out 1,200 pieces an hour. Fish and chips predated McDonald's in Britain by a century. North American Indians had *pemmican.*

Did America Invent Fast Food?

The idea that Americans invented fast food would be hilariously ethnocentric if it were not so widely believed outside the United States. Equally uncritical is the notion that United States fast food *causes* foreigners to eat faster than they used to. The Japanese have always eaten lunch quickly, and Mexicans are no laggards. Many Europeans simply skip lunch. Some cultures eat faster than Americans do, and some eat more slowy. The pace is governed by factors other than proximity to the golden arches.

Yet there are professors asserting that McDonald's caused the demise of sit-down dining in Japan. A strange charge, since for more than a hundred years Japanese has had words for eating while standing (*tachikui*) and drinking while standing (*tachinomi*). In fact, the oldest bars in Japan are the *tachinomiya* (place to drink standing up), and all railroad stations have had standup *ramen* shops since at least World War II. Historic accounts, drawings, and photos show that the Japanese ate while standing in the street in the 1880s.

Everyone, of course, feels a right to weigh in on the fast-food debate—after all, they eat it!—but almost no one goes out and studies eating. And critics in the United States do not recognize the increase in foreign foods that they themselves eat, tastes that began to return with those backpackers in the 1960s: *tom yum* sauce from Thailand, *fleur du sel* [gourmet salt] from the French Camargue, Jamaican rum, and Italian tomatoes. Augmented by increased incomes and personal mo-

- Half of McDonald's dollars come from window sales, but auto traffic requires more land and parking lots and high-tech order systems. These are more labor intensive and costly than counter sales.

- In 2000 there were about 12,000 McDonald's in the United States, and 8,000 in eighty-nine other countries. There are 1,482 *Makudos* in Japan (by far the largest foreign presence), 430 in France, 63 in China, 2 in Bulgaria, and 2 in Andorra. These were owned mostly by foreign franchisees.

- As for Beijing, only 10 percent of the Chinese population can afford to buy a Big Mac, by McDonald's estimates. The company is there because it wants a foothold in the world's largest market.

- McDonald's spends about $1 billion a year on worldwide advertising. In the 1990s, most of that went for television ads shot by Leo Burnett and DDB Needham in an upbeat "Steven Spielberg style." This advertising is not localized, often produced abroad, and probably less effective than it should be. Its ineffectuality is a sore spot with McDonald's shareholders and franchisees.

- McDonald's customers are *very* picky and attempts to win them to new products fail more often than they succeed. The McLean Deluxe, introduced in 1991 because U.S. critics carped about fat, was a major failure. "People talk thin but they eat fat," says senior vice-president Richard Starrman.

gely Localized Business

aps the biggest misconception is that McDonald's is the an horse of American ideology. But golden arches out do not translate to "American" inside, as even its critics "McDonald's adapts to each distinctive cultural context

bility, American tastes led the way to a *modern* pr
a more diverse food palate, which has since spread
of the world. But this modernization has not bee
nied by the spread of "American" flavors. As for
it has succeeded abroad largely for the same rea
has succeeded at home.

Perhaps the biggest misconception is that McD
the Trojan horse of American ideology.

McDonald's tried a "store" (to use company
Holland in 1960, which failed, and then another
1967, which succeeded. It opened its first Jap
1970, and by 1980 it had four hundred there,
known as "Makudo." By year 2000 there were f
France. In Italy, home of the "slow food" mov
Italians a day were eating at three hundred
2003. That is actually not very many. . . .

McDonald's in Context

Here are some statistics from a profile by Ste
the *New York Times* that help to put McDon
tive.

- Only 7 percent of the U.S. population
  and this might be only for a cup of co

- McDonald's accounted for only 15.2 p
  food sold in the United States in 2002
  peak of 18 percent in the late 1980s.

- In 2003 the typical customer was a m
  teens to early 30s, who ate there twic
  counted for 75 percent of McDonald
  and he expects—really!—to be served
  minute, though the company meets
  only about half the time. He is, obvi
  slice of the U.S. population.

Lar

Perl

Tro

fron

note

and, as a result, is so modified that it is ultimately impossible to distinguish the local from the foreign. Thus, in China McDonald's is seen as much a Chinese phenomenon as it is an American phenomenon. In Japan McDonald's is perceived by some as *Americana as constructed* by the Japanese." Though not a critic, Thomas Friedman made the same point when he noted a Japanese child visiting the United States who was surprised to learn that there were McDonald's here. This is an aspect of what James L. Watson has termed the "transnationality" phenomenon, in which a company becomes a federation of semiautonomous enterprises.

But even transnationality has limits. McDonald's franchisees may add beer in Germany, salsa in Mexico, and soy flavors in Japan, but the essence of McDonald's is its process and logistics. It always has low prices, a clean dining room, efficient service, polite staff, good lighting, lots and lots of free seating, even for noncustomers, and free, clean bathrooms. This may seem obvious to Americans, but in much of the world this is revolutionary. In the rest of the world one simply does not enter a restaurant without buying something, much less use the toilets (for free!)—cleanliness in the latter would be iffy anyway. There are certainly no free seats for doing homework, as in the Nishinomiya Makudo. Even Ritzer and Malone concede that "in both Hong Kong and Taipei McDonald's virtually invented restaurant cleanliness and served as a catalyst for improving sanitary conditions at many other restaurants in the city." The same is true across Europe, not to mention Mexico and South America.

Like a classic French restaurant, McDonald's allows customers to stay as long as they want. When I taught in Vienna in 1993–94, McDonald's had to raise the price of its coffee to the level of Viennese *Kaffeehäuser*, because the latter complained. It seems that elderly *omas*, who were hustled rudely out of the local Meinl coffee shops, discovered they could spend an afternoon at McD. In Mexico, Japan, France, Taiwan, and Poland, I've seen teenagers hang out at McDonald's after school for hours, doing homework or talking. Travelers stop in to read undisturbed, businessmen to call home or telecompute via cell phones. All this in a "clean, well-lighted place"— Hemingway's old man knew how rare they were. It is a value of modernity that is appreciated worldwide.

McDonald's Sets Standards

On one hand McDonald's is accused of standardizing international taste. But aren't clean, free bathrooms a good standard? On the other, when critics discover that McDonald's alters its menu to suit local tastes, it is accused of an insidious capitalist plot: McDonald's "impact is far greater it if infiltrates a local culture and becomes a part of it than if it remains perceived as an American phenomenon superimposed on a local setting," write Ritzer and Malone.

> *[Foreign] entrepreneurs have caught on quickly, blending more local cuisine with fast food's speed, modernity, and service.*

Few critics realize that the chain's great successes, from the Egg McMuffin to the Big Mac, sprang from *local* franchisees, who are encouraged to experiment. And foreign franchisees are not getting hamburger from America; they have to find local suppliers as soon as possible, buying their meat and potatoes, their milk and buns in the area. McDonald's of Austria even taught farmers in Poland and Slovakia how to raise the low-water-content potatoes used in McDonald's fries. McDonald's franchises in Austria buy 90 percent of their ingredients in central Europe.

But there are a dozen other American fast-food chains abroad. As Thomas Frank wrote in the *New York Times*:

> Even more adaptive in terms of food are the smaller American food franchisers (Big Boy, Dairy Queen, Schlotzsky's

Delicatessen, and Chesapeake Bagel) that have followed McDonald's and the other American giants overseas. In 1990, alone, these mini-chains opened 800 new restaurants overseas and as of that year there were more than 12,000 of them in existence around the world. However such mini-chains are far weaker than McDonald's and therefore must be even more responsive to local culture. Thus, Big Boy sells things like "country-style fried rice and pork omelet" and has added sugar and chili powder to make its burgers more palatable to its Thai customers. Because it caters to many European tourists, it has added Germanic foods like spätzle to its menu. Said the head franchiser for Big Boy in Thailand: "We thought we were bringing American food to the masses. . . . But now we're bringing Thai and European food to the tourists."

Local Cultures Adapt

Local entrepreneurs have caught on quickly, blending more local cuisine with fast food's speed, modernity, and service. In China there are three imitators of KFC alone: Ronghua Chicken, Xiangfei Roast Chicken, and Beijing Fast Food Company. The founders of the latter used to work for McDonald's and KFC.

If we return to the Nishinomiya train station, we can see a Moos Burger (1,500 outlets in Japan), which serves a sloppy-joe concoction, and a Yoshinoya, which serves traditional Japanese food fast (more than 2,000 outlets—more than McDonald's!). In three minutes Yoshinoya serves up a salmon filet, vegetables, rice, pickles, and tea for $4.50. In 1979 it opened its first U.S. shop, and there were sixty-two in Los Angeles County by 2003, with plans for a thousand nationwide.

In Russia there is Russkoye Bistro, which has more than a hundred outlets and serves 35,000 to 40,000 customers per day. "If McDonald's had not come to our country," says Russkoye's deputy director, "Then we probably wouldn't be here. We need to create fast food here that fits our lifestyle and traditions.... We see McDonald's like an older brother.... We have a lot to learn from them." When I visited impoverished Latvia just after the Iron Curtain lifted, there was one McDonald's with three local imitators. The most successful was called "Little Johnny's," run by former employees of McDonald's, and it was doing a better business than its older brother....

Encouraging Values

There are other values associated with fast food that we might wish to see more of abroad. By now it is a cliché to speak of the way in which the industry socializes youth to the workplace; provides opportunities for minorities, the handicapped, and older citizens; or sponsors local charities and fund raisers. But it is worth noting that the family-owned "greasy spoon" of yore did none of these. It did not promote sexual equality in the workplace, nondiscrimination, handicapped access, or corporate charity. These ideals, where practiced overseas by McDonald's and its imitators, cynically or not, are new to most developing nations and some European ones. Fairness, compassion, and meritocracy are still a tough sell abroad, however, and are widely resisted, ignored, or resented.

All facts considered, the McDonald's brouhaha is more about image than substance.

Critics also fail to understand that most fast-food franchises are locally owned. Most of the profit, power, and experience stay abroad. McDonald's selects locations, based on human and vehicle traffic and other considerations. It trains franchisees extensively, then offers them locations. McDonald's owns the land, so there is no chance for franchisee self-dealing in real estate. Its real-estate acumen offers McDonald's as much opportunity for profit as its cut of the franchisee's sales; indeed, to Russia's risky realty market McDonald's has brought traffic analysis and other sophisticated tools now copied by locals. The franchisee must install exactly the shop that McDonald's stipulates and go to work in it full-time. Hands-on management is the norm. These are radically different practices from those that prevail in most of the underdeveloped world. The result is that some urban franchises make $2,000 an hour during peak lunch periods. As for food quality, McDonald's operates an extensive customer feedback and complaint system. There is less than one complaint about food per store per year worldwide, and only three about service. The facilities themselves receive a minuscule number of complaints, according to Drucker.

Saddest of all, critics don't realize that McDonald's is not the world's largest fast-food company. That honor goes to the Compass Group of Great Britain, which owns Burger King, Sbarro, and a host of other brands. Compass serves more airports, company lunchrooms, and school cafeterias than any other company, but it has no single, recognizable logo. McDonald's is second, followed closely by the French firm Sodexho. It seems that while some Frenchmen are criticizing the golden arches, other Frenchmen have a $1 billion a year contract to serve food fast to the U.S. Marine Corps, the UN forces in Kosovo, and American forces in Iraq. In fact Sodexho employs 110,000 Americans; it's a global power, even a colonial one. McDonald's employs only 35,000 French. All facts considered, the McDonald's brouhaha is more about image than substance.

Organizations to Contact

The editors have compiled the following list of organizations concerned with the issues debated in this book. The descriptions are derived from materials provided by the organizations. All have publications or information available for interested readers. The list was compiled on the date of publication of the present volume; the information provided here may change. Be aware that many organizations take several weeks or longer to respond to inquiries, so allow as much time as possible.

Food and Society
W.K. Kellogg Foundation, East Battle Creek, MI   49017-4012
(269) 968-1611 • fax: (269) 968-0413
Web site: www.wkkf.org

Launched in 2000, Food and Society is based on a vision of a future food system that provides all segments of society a safe and nutritious food supply, grown in a manner that protects health and the environment and adds economic and social value to rural and urban communities.

Humane Farm Animal Care
PO Box 727, Herndon, VA   20172
Web site: www.certifiedhumane.com

Humane Farm Animal Care is a nonprofit animal welfare certification organization. The organization certifies and labels meat, eggs, dairy, and poultry products, guaranteeing that such items were produced according to the organization's animal-care standards. Humane Farm Animal Care's Web site includes a fact sheet on animal-care standards and procedures.

National Association to Advance Fat Acceptance (NAAFA)
PO Box 22510, Oakland, CA   94609
(916) 558-6880
Web site: www.naafaonline.com

Founded in 1969, NAAFA is a nonprofit civil rights organization dedicated to ending size discrimination in all of its forms. NAAFA's goal is to help build a society in which people of every size are accepted with dignity and equality in all aspects of life. The organization pursues this goal through advocacy, public education, and support.

People for the Ethical Treatment of Animals (PETA)
501 Front St., Norfolk, VA   23510
(757) 622-PETA (7382) • fax: (757) 622-0457
Web site: www.peta.org

PETA, with more than 2 million members and supporters, is the largest animal rights organization in the world. PETA focuses its attention on the four areas in which the largest numbers of animals suffer the most intensely for the longest periods of time: on factory farms, in laboratories, in the clothing trade, and in the entertainment industry. The organization effects its goals through public education, cruelty investigations, research, animal rescue, legislation, special events, celebrity involvement, and protest campaigns.

Slow Food International
Piazza XX Settembre, 5, Bra (Cuneo), Italy   12042
+39 0172 419611 • fax: +39 0172 421293
e-mail: international@slowfood.com
Web site: www.slowfood.com

Slow Food is a nonprofit, eco-gastronomic member-supported organization that was founded in 1989. The organization works to support biodiversity in the food supply, to counteract what it describes as "fast food and fast life," and to reawaken the appreciation for high-quality, traditional, locally produced food. The organization publishes *Slow Food Times*, a monthly online magazine.

Socially Accountable Farm Employers (SAFE)
PO Box 940926, Maitland, FL   32794-0926
Web site: www.safeagemployer.org

SAFE provides independent, third-party certification of labor practices for farm employers. Recognizing the growing need for social accountability by farm employers, SAFE was formed in 2005 by the Redlands Christian Migrant Association and the Florida Fruit & Vegetable Association.

U.S. Food and Drug Administration (FDA)
5600 Fishers Lane, Rockville, Maryland   20857
(888) INFO-FDA (463-6332)
Web site: www.fda.gov

The FDA is one of the nation's oldest consumer protection agencies. Its mission is to promote and protect the public health by helping safe and effective products reach the market in a timely way, monitor products for continued safety after they are in use, and help the public get the accurate, science-based information needed to improve health. Its Web site features links to numerous speeches, articles, and congressional testimonies.

Bibliography

Books

Paul Campos · *The Diet Myth: Why America's Obsession with Weight Is Hazardous to Your Health.* New York: Gotham, 2006.

Autumn Libel · *Fats, Sugars, and Empty Calories: The Fast Food Habit.* Philadelphia: Mason Crest, 2006.

Gina Mallet · *Last Chance to Eat: The Fate of Taste in a Fast Food World.* New York: Norton, 2004.

J. Eric Oliver · *Fat Politics: The Real Story Behind America's Obesity Epidemic.* New York: Oxford University Press, 2006.

George Ritzer · *McDonaldization of Society 5.* Los Angeles: Pine Forge, 2008.

Eric Schlosser · *Fast Food Nation: The Dark Side of the All-American Meal.* New York: HarperPerennial, 2005.

Eric Schlosser and Charles Wilson · *Chew on This: Everything You Don't Want to Know About Fast Food.* Boston: Houghton Mifflin, 2006.

Michele Simon · *Appetite for Profit: How the Food Industry Undermines Our Health and How to Fight Back.* New York: Nation Books, 2006.

Andrew F. Smith	*Encyclopedia of Junk and Fast Food.* Westport, CT: Greenwood, 2006.
Morgan Spurlock	*Don't Eat This Book: Fast Food and the Supersizing of America.* New York: G.P. Putnam's Sons, 2005.
Jennifer Parker Talwar	*Fast Food, Fast Track: Immigrants, Big Business, and the American Dream.* Boulder, CO: Westview, 2003.
Tina Volpe	*The Fast Food Craze: Wreaking Havoc on Our Bodies and Our Animals.* Kagel Canyon, CA: Canyon, 2005.

Periodicals

Frank Bruni	"Life in the Fast-Food Lane," *New York Times*, May 24, 2006.
Steve Chapman	"Force-Fed the Facts," *Reason*, June 23, 2008.
Temple Grandin	"Special Report: Maintenance of Good Animal Welfare in Beef Slaughter Plants by Use of Auditing Programs," *Journal of the American Veterinary Medical Association*, February 1, 2005.
Anne Kingston and Nicholas Kohler	"L.A.'s Fast Food Drive-by: A City Council's Ban on Fast-Food Chains Is a Provocative Social Experiment," *Maclean's*, August 25, 2008.
Laura Kipnis	"America's Waistline," *Slate*, October 28, 2005. www.slate.com.

Amelia Levin	"Good Food Fast," *Foodservice Equipment & Supplies*, October 1, 2006.
Sarah More McCann	"Wanted: Inner-City Supermarkets," *Christian Science Monitor*, June 27, 2008.
Ruth Mortimer	"Why Fast-Food Brands Should Not Change Their Recipe for Success," *Marketing Week*, August 28, 2008.
Evelyn Nieves	"Fla. Tomato Pickers Still Reap 'Harvest of Shame,'" *Washington Post*, February 28, 2005.
Jennifer Ordoñez	"Fast-Food Lovers, Unite!" *Newsweek*, May 24, 2004.
Jonathan Rosenblum	"Fast Food Nation Interview: Eric Schlosser on Obesity, Kids, and Fast-Food PR," *PR Watch*, November 17, 2006. www.prwatch.org.
Gary Ruskin and Juliet Schor	"Junk Food Nation," *Nation*, August 29, 2005.
William Saletan	"Junk-Food Jihad," *Slate*, April 15, 2006. www.slate.com.
San Francisco Chronicle	"Battle of the Bulge: Fast Food Is King at Arroyo High," June 29, 2003.
Morgan Spurlock	"The Truth About McDonald's and Children," *Independent* (London), May 22, 2005.

Index